# DON'T RELY ON GEMINI

## *Vin Packer*

PROLOGUE BOOKS

F+W Media, Inc.

Published in electronic format by
PROLOGUE BOOKS
an imprint of F+W Media, Inc.
10151 Carver Road
Blue Ash, Ohio 45242
*www.prologuebooks.com*



eISBN 10: 1-4405-3704-6
eISBN 13: 978-1-4405-3704-2

POD ISBN 10: 1-4405-5611-3
POD ISBN 13: 978-1-4405-5611-1



This work has been previously published in print format by:
Delacorte Press.

FOR VIVIAN SCHULTE,

A CAPRICORN,

AND A VERY DEAR FRIEND,

WITH THANKS.

DON'T RELY ON GEMINI

CHAPTER 1

He was thinking of Liddy again.

Mrs. Muckermann said, "You're not really listening to me, Archie."

"I'm sorry. My mind wandered for a moment."

A woman at the next table was smoking a Gauloise, as Liddy always had. The strong scent of the cigarette reminded Archie of her. He even put on his glasses to be sure it was not Liddy, though he knew the last place in New York City where he would find her would be in this basement tearoom on Irving Place.

It was called the Singing Tea Kettle: good homemade food, no bar, no air-conditioning; but everyone there knew Anna Muckermann. The old English sea captain who owned the place often stopped by her table to discuss astrology with her. The teachers and other customers who worked in the neighborhood and lunched there sometimes asked her questions: would a Pisces get along with a Capricorn; what was someone born under Taurus like; if you were born at midnight on July 22, were you Cancer or Leo?

Mrs. Muckermann enjoyed the attention. But when she

was unhappy she complained that everyone wanted something for nothing, and she was tired of having her brain picked. Did people stop a doctor in a restaurant and ask him about their symptoms?

Today was one of those days. There were no gracious smiles for anyone, no small talk between tables, and she was impatient with Archie. Even before he had started thinking of Liddy, Mrs. Muckermann had been in a bad mood. She was not pleased with his progress on the CBS special about her.

"We need more substance!" she had told Archie. "I will not come off as a quack, no better than a gypsy fortune-teller!"

Archie was the writer for the show. He seldom worked in television, and he knew nothing about astrology. He was a novelist, and he wrote short stories and nonfiction pieces for magazines. This assignment was a fluke. When he and Dru had moved into the Gramercy area, Dru had managed to get a key to the private park. There she had struck up a friendship with Mrs. Muckermann. When CBS approached Mrs. Muckermann about doing an hour-long examination of a modern-day astrologer, she agreed on the condition that Archie Gamble would write the script.

After Mrs. Muckermann finished her chocolate pudding, she said, "Archie, I know why you're distracted, but you *can* fight these things, you know."

He didn't answer. He was suddenly furious with Dru. He imagined that she had told Mrs. Muckermann that Liddy was back in New York. He could just hear it, picture it.

—He never got over her, Mrs. Muckermann. I met Archie when their marriage was breaking up, and he was some mess! You wouldn't *believe* it!

The two of them, no doubt, in their little private park, which Archie hated because it had an iron fence all the way around it. Only The Privileged received keys to get inside.

—Well, Druscilla, Archie *is* a Gemini. You can't rely on Gemini. I always say that. You can't.

—He wouldn't leave me, go back to her?

—You can't predict a Gemini. But I'd have to see his current aspects again, review them, to give you a better prognosis.

That was the way it probably went.

Archie frowned and dug into his gingerbread, irritated now because when he was with Mrs. Muckermann it was always at a place where he couldn't get a drink, and invariably, at some point during these sessions, he wanted one.

Mrs. Muckermann said, "Or aren't you a fighter?"

"What?"

"I said you can fight these things. Are you a fighter?"

"What does Dru say?"

"I don't know that Dru's aware of it."

He said, "What are you talking about?"

He was no longer sure himself.

"I'm talking about the reason you're distracted," said Mrs. Muckermann. "Mercury and Saturn are stimulating an opposition in your chart."

Archie smiled, relieved that she hadn't meant Liddy was distracting him. "So that's it," he said.

"I pointed it out to you last week. It's a bad aspect."

"When will it be over, Mrs. Muckermann?"

"It'll be there through 1974. But it's very strong now."

"I'm going to be distracted until 1974?" He chuckled.

"Off and on, yes. Worse than that. You'll be compulsive, at times heartless. Self-concerned. But you can fight it. You have Jupiter working for you, Archie. It's a very lucky planet. It saw Pope John through. It was a strong influence in his horoscope, too."

"Was Pope John a Gemini?"

"Oh, no. No, Archie. He was a Sagittarius." She wiped her mouth with her napkin and gathered her pocketbook from the floor. She was always ready to rush out of a restaurant after she finished her dessert, whether or not Archie had finished his. She studied her reflection in her compact while he gulped down the rest of his gingerbread. She was a short, thin little stick-legged woman who looked like a bird with enormous blue eyes. "Geminis," she said, "don't often rise to positions of power. And if they do, they don't last long in them. We've had only one Gemini president."

Archie reached for the check. "Who was that?"

"John Kennedy," said Mrs. Muckermann flatly.

Mrs. Muckermann lived in the Gramercy Park Hotel, and Archie walked her there, lingering with her for a few minutes in the lobby while she registered more complaints about the material for the show.

"I'm most disappointed," she said, "about your failure to locate at least one pair of astro-twins."

Astro-twins were people who had not only the same birth-date, but also the same hour and minute of birth, and were born in the same longitude and latitude.

Archie said, "I've already spent a few hundred dollars advertising for them."

The ads had been placed in the *Times, The Saturday Review, The Village Voice* and *Variety*. Archie had even persuaded a reporter from the New York *Post* to write an article about the search. They had chosen twenty-five people from CBS, published their dates, places, and times of birth, and asked anyone with a matching date, place, and time to call a special number or write to a box listing. There had been no answers.

Mrs. Muckermann said, "A few hundred dollars isn't enough."

"I can't go over the budget."

"Then we should have a bigger budget. Astro-twins prove the validity of astrology. In one hundred percent of the cases investigated in England, we found that these people live parallel lives."

"Absolutely?"

"No, not absolutely, Archie. You have to make allowances for genetic differences and differences in the stations or positions into which they were born. But their similarities are breathtaking. Didn't you read the Goodavage book I lent you?"

"Not all of it."

Not any of it. There just wasn't time to read everything Mrs. Muckermann had lent him. This show couldn't become his life's work, much as she wanted it to be.

She said, "You didn't read any of it. Mr. Goodavage began the book with a discussion of astro-twins."

"I don't remember. I've read so much on the subject lately."

"You'd remember if you'd read it," she said. "You'd remember cases like Samuel Hemmings and King George IV."

"They were astro-twins?"

"Yes, indeed. Hemmings was a commoner, an ironmonger. On the very same day that George IV ascended to the throne, Hemmings went into business for himself."

"Ummm. Impressive."

"Don't be cynical with me. I know too much about you. Your vulnerabilities and Saturn's influence in your chart," said Mrs. Muckermann. "Hemmings was married on the same day the King was. Each became ill and had accidents at the same times. Their successes and failures matched, and their personalities were very similar. They died in the same hour of the same day of the same cause."

Archie said, "Is it possible for it to be authenticated?"

"Of course. Every book on the subject mentions it. There's a vast amount of research material on it."

"Then we could write it into the show."

"Oh, there's so much material on astro-twins. We could write it all into the show," said Mrs. Muckermann sighing heavily, "but I want living proof, contemporary proof. It'll take more than a few hundred dollars to come up with it, but it'll be worth it."

Archie shook his head. "No way . . . the budget is set."

"Then CBS will have a flop on their hands!"

"Not exactly a unique experience for CBS," said Archie.

"But it would be for me, you see," Mrs. Muckermann answered, "which is the very reason I'm contemplating withdrawing my participation. I'm perfectly serious, Archie."

He knew she was. He knew, too, that without her the show would go on, that CBS would find another astrologer . . . and another writer. He had put two months into this project already, and been paid only two thousand dollars down on the guaranteed ten thousand for the finished script.

"Mrs. Muckermann," Archie said, smiling unhappily, "I thought I had Jupiter working for me."

"Only if you fight, dear boy."

He knew what Dru would say when he went home and told her that Mrs. Muckermann was beginning to give him a hard time.

He wasn't ready for it, so he went to Pete's Restaurant on the corner of 18th Street and Irving Place and ordered a beer.

Dru would say, "I don't *believe* her!"

Or, "Are you *ready* for this?"

Her stock sayings with the stock emphases on certain words. She always picked up all the current New York jargon, something Liddy would never do. Liddy would never imitate anyone. What she said, what she wore, the way she was, were unmistakably Lydia Denyven.

—Liddy, I'm worried that I'll lose this show.

—Then you don't need it, Archie. You don't need anything that makes you worry. I won't let you worry.

He swallowed some of his beer and laughed weakly to himself at the idea of Liddy not letting him worry. Yeah, right. If worry was motion, he had spent most of his marriage to Liddy in a state of perpetual motion.

Liddy wouldn't pick up any jargon or fads, but she had never been too fussy about other pickups.

Well, what are you going to do with a Scorpio? As that old

philosopher Mrs. Muckermann would say: passions flow through Scorpio. In Mrs. Muckermann's studio there was an asexual marble nude sitting atop a gold pedestal. Small labels pointed out the parts of the body ruled by the signs of the Zodiac. Above the toes was the symbol for Pisces and the word "feet." Under the chin was the symbol for Taurus and the word "neck." Above the heart was the symbol for Cancer and the word "breast." Next to it was the symbol for Leo and the word "heart." There was Sagittarius on the thighs, Capricorn on the knees, Aquarius on the legs, etc. And there between the legs was the symbol for Scorpio and Mrs. Muckermann's subtle description: "secrets."

Go win.

Archie took another pull on his beer and decided the hell with Liddy. So she was back. God, how he loved theatrics, walking in the rain last night, remember, with his coat collar pulled up, cigarette in his mouth, brooding, thinking of himself walking in the rain at night with his coat collar pulled up, cigarette in his mouth, recalling Liddy's voice, body, thinking of her seeing him that way, one of her friends seeing him that way, remember?

—He must know you're back, darling. He looked so melancholy.

Wasn't he a little middle-aged now for these melodramatics?

He was suddenly almost forty-two, the same way he had suddenly become twenty-one, and then thirty; did it happen so fast to everyone?

Not Dru.

Dru was dying to be older.

She was twenty-seven. She had no memories of bobbysocks or butter rationing or phonograph records that broke if you dropped them, or rumble seats or saddle shoes or a skyline unmolested by television aerials or the sovereign state of Lithuania.

She was Cancer, or as Mrs. Muckermann preferred to call anyone with that sun sign, a Moon Child.

What was that little poem Mrs. Muckermann recited about Cancer/Moon Children?

> Who changes like a changeful season,
> Holds fast and lets go without reason?
> Who is there can give adhesion
> To Cancer?

"*Cherchez la mère*," Mrs. Muckermann was fond of quoting the French astrologer Barbault on the subject of Cancer, "*et vous trouverez le Cancer!*"

But Dru always said, "The last thing I want is to have a baby. I guess I'm too selfish. I just never wanted to be a mother."

Good.

Neither did Archie want children any more. (Liddy had wanted them so badly!)

"How can I buy this astrological mishmash, though?" Archie had complained to Dru shortly after he accepted the CBS assignment. "I like to have at least a little enthusiasm for my work. It's impossible with this subject."

Dru had said, "Concentrate on the historical aspects, Arch. You know, how that seventeenth-century Englishman foretold London's Great Fire of 1666—what was his name? Lee?"

"William Lilly. But this is a show about contemporary astrology."

"Then mention the fact that the Crown Prince of Sikkim and that Hope Cooke postponed their wedding for a year because the astrologers told them to. Things like that."

"Dru," Archie had answered, "I have to get down to the nitty-gritty. Leos are lionlike and Pisceans are mystical, and you Cancers are whacked out because the moon rules you."

She had said, "I'm not whacked out. I'm Rita Reliable, and you know it."

She was, too.

He could not envision her changing like a changeful season, or letting go without a reason, or any of it.

"Hi!" he said, hugging her in their foyer. "I missed you."

"Damnit all, Archie, you stopped for a beer!" She pushed him away and walked toward the kitchen, looking more than usual today like Julie Harris fifteen years ago. He followed her. He came up behind her and put his arms around her. "Since when am I disallowed a draft or two at the corner bar?"

"You spoiled the surprise," she said, taking the Waring blender's pitcher off its stand "Remember the banana daiquiris we had at Wednesday's Saturday night?"

"Now? At two in the afternoon?"

"They're like a dessert. I made them very thick. But the beer taste will spoil it."

"When did we start drinking after lunch?"

"We'll have them in those long-stemmed blue champagne glasses," she said. "Reach above you in the cupboard."

He reached. He said, "Oh, we started drinking after lunch about a year ago, Archie. That's how we became lushes."

"I don't care if you have had beer. These will be delicious." He handed her the glasses.

"We're going to have twins, darling," she said.

"What the hell are you talking about?"

"I'm talking about astro-twins. Archie, we got an answer! We've located an astro-twin, right over near Nyack!"

"You're kidding! Whose?"

She handed him the pitcher. "Yours. Pour. I'll get the letter."

"*Mine?*"

"His name is Neal Dana. He was born on May twenty-seventh, 1927, in New York City, at three-thirty A.M. Same date, same place, same time. Just different hospitals."

He stood there with his mouth hanging open, holding the pitcher of banana daiquiris.

"Take the drinks out on the terrace, Arch," she called after him. "We'll celebrate there."

It was the first Monday in May.

CHAPTER 2

"Neal? Where are you?"

"I'm in a gas station on Route 9W. Penny, I've got good news!"

"Did you see the Doubleday editor?"

"Yes. He likes the idea, Pen. He really likes it!"

"Will they publish it?"

"I'm going to do an outline for him."

"Oh, Neal, I'm so excited!"

"I think I can get a contract and an advance."

"Really?"

"Not much of an advance."

"Darling, that would really make it official, wouldn't it?"

"I probably won't get more than a thousand dollars."

"It's not the money, Neal."

"I know."

"You're going to be famous, Neal. I feel it!"

He laughed. "Hold on. I've got to write the book first."

"Don't laugh," she said. "Some night I'll turn on my television and there you'll be on Johnny Carson."

"Sure. Uh huh."

"Just like that doctor who wrote *Games People Play*."

10

"Oh, Pen, my stuff isn't that commercial."

"Who says so? I think it's fascinating."

"I've got to write the book first. Maybe I can't even write a book."

"You wrote a thesis . . . Oh, Neal, I wish we could see each other tonight."

"Wednesday's not far away. Margaret will be going into New York for her Italian class."

"Who says it's not far away? Neal, I *miss* you."

"Then stop by the clinic tomorrow and pick me up for lunch."

"Do you mean it?"

"Around twelve-thirty."

"I love you, Neal."

"I love *you*, Penny."

Did he?

Neal Dana took a right off 9W and drove his English Ford Consul down a winding hill into the town of Piermont, New York. Then he swung onto River Road, heading for Grandview-on-Hudson, in between Piermont and Nyack.

Dr. Dana (Ph.D.) was a psychologist attached to the Rock-Or clinic in Nyack. It was a private clinic, primarily an out-patient setup, but there were resident patients in the thirty-bed hospital, and seven private cottages on the grounds housing three patients each.

Rockland Countyites called it "Wethead Haven" because of the high percentage of alcoholics treated there, but the clinic had its share of catatonics, paranoids, and other schizophrenics, as well as miscellaneous neurotics who were teetering on the brink of psychosis.

It was an expensive clinic. Until a year ago, Rock-Or accepted no charity cases. Largely through Neal's efforts the rule had been relaxed to admit a few in residence and many more for consultation.

Penny's brother, Forrest Bissel, a chronic petty larcenist with a prison record, had been one of the first charity patients assigned to Neal. Forrest was twenty-two, one year younger than Penny. Both of them had been "battered children," or children who had been beaten by one or more adults—in Penny's and Forrest's case, by Clarence Bissel, their father.

Penny still lived with her father in a small apartment in downtown Nyack. The mother was dead. Forrest had a room in Piermont, where he worked for Continental Can.

If Neal Dana had rehabilitated Forrest Bissel, Penny Bissel had rehabilitated Neal Dana. She had changed him from a middle-aged psychologist with the bitter regret that he was not an M.D. to a young man in his early forties who was just beginning to realize his potential as a therapist. And a writer —there was that now, too. Penny had convinced him that his long study of the psychological meaning of everyday mannerisms could be made into an interesting book.

On this first Monday in May he had finally done something about it.

He would have liked to celebrate this small triumph over his own self-doubts. He would choose to celebrate it by buying a bottle of champagne and enjoying a leisurely dinner while he detailed the day's happenings, then brandy on the upper porch overlooking the Hudson, watching the lights of traffic on the graceful, low-slung Tappan Zee bridge and the shore lights of Tarrytown . . . then bed, and the easy, warm lovemaking of two people a little high and awfully happy.

But Margaret was on a perpetual diet and refused to "waste calories" on alcohol. She never cleared the table before he was finished, but she always sat there politely, impatient to clear; she ate quickly and talked very little during a meal. Afterward she always had a project to attend to: something she was learning, or fixing, or beginning, or finally getting around to. They made love often, but not for long any more. Horizontally, Margaret was not very much different from the way she was vertically. She was efficient, controlled, and courteous.

She never failed to brush her teeth and gargle when it was over.

The house was at the top of a long, winding hill. It was small, more like a cottage, yellow with white shutters and a certain precious dollhouse look to it. Red roses climbed a trellis along one side. It was encircled by woods, and behind it was a small, round swimming pool, a white wooden summer house with built-in benches, and Margaret's extensive vegetable garden and flowerbeds.

Neal Dana shifted gears for the steep climb and honked his horn as the sign at the bottom of the hill directed, to warn anyone starting down that you were starting up. The neighbors' new Doberman pinscher came snarling across their wide lawn to give chase to the car.


"How did it go, dear?" Margaret's new brown dress matched her hair.

"Fine!" he said. "I'm going to do an outline."

"Marvelous, Neal! . . . Do you want plain squash with your steak, or squash with onions and tomatoes?"

"Oh, I don't care." He put his briefcase on a chair and looked at his mail. "I wish Minnie Nickerson would do something about her dog."

"Decide how you want your squash. The coals are ready, dear."

"It's only quarter to six, Margaret."

"Do you mind awfully? I have my language records to work on after dinner, and I want to finish the Goodavage book."

"Will I have time for a shower?"

"A quick one. Don't putter, Neal."

He left the bill from Abercrombie unopened. He had ordered a velours shirt from there for Penny. Margaret paid the bills, but she never opened anything addressed to him. He would sneak the envelope into his briefcase at some point and send a check from the office.

It had been risky to charge and send that way. The receiver's name and address were probably marked across the sales slip. Neal realized it had been too risky to be accidental; a part of him wanted Margaret to know, was inviting a showdown.

Not yet.

It was too soon. He had only known Penny for six months. There was a twenty-year age difference. There was his position at Rock-Or. There were nineteen years of marriage. There was—Lord, so very much involved. What was he doing, anyway, even thinking about Penny and himself that way?

"Plain squash or squash with onions and tomatoes?" Margaret asked.

"I don't care."

"Which one?"

"Plain squash."

"Well, you don't have to bite my head off, Neal."

There was always a clean cloth on the table, and linen napkins.

"No pieces with fat on them, dear," Margaret said, passing him her plate.

He served her some of the charcoaled steak, a helping of squash, and some new potatoes.

"Put three potatoes back, dear . . . Tell me what the editor said."

"I'm going to do an outline."

"Neal, I *said* put three back."

"I put two back. You're not going to eat just one little potato?"

"Put the other back. I *am* going to eat just one."

"All right, here."

"Thank you."

"I think I'll get a contract and an advance."

"I couldn't be more pleased."

"Not much of an advance. A thousand dollars, fifteen hundred."

"That isn't much, is it?"

"They don't pay much."

"Doubleday? They're one of the biggest publishing houses in the world."

"Publishers in general. They don't pay much."

"Dear, they *do* pay considerably more than that. I read where they paid Harold Robbins something like four hundred thousand for just an idea."

"Margaret, I'm not Harold Robbins. I'm not Jacqueline Susann, either."

"There ought to be a happy medium between one thousand and four hundred thousand all the same."

"They pay more for novels."

"I wonder what they paid for *Our Crowd?*"

"It isn't the money that's important, is it?"

She looked across at him and smiled, closed her eyes and opened them, and said, "Of course not."

Margaret always winked with both eyes at the same time. As much as Neal had studied the psychological importance of everyday mannerisms, that was one of Margaret's everyday gestures he couldn't figure out. Was she begging "enough!" in a very civilized way, or indicating that when she opened her eyes whatever it was that had been there before she closed them, wouldn't be there any more?

The latter, perhaps, for she was changing the subject now.

"There's something missing, and you haven't even commented on it."

But he wanted to talk about what had happened at Doubleday. He said, "Of course the thousand wouldn't be all I'd get if the book were successful."

"Don't you wonder where Sinister is?"

Sinister was their parrot. He amused Neal, but Neal could

live without him. He required live worms in his diet, which Margaret kept in a jar in the refrigerator, and if he felt left out of things he whistled and sang at the top of his lungs and called out, "I'm Sinister! I love the view!"

"Where is he?" Neal said.

Margaret broke into baby talk. "Him's at the vet's. Him is getting a pedicure and him's getting a dip, and him has to stay overnight."

It was totally un-Margaret to speak that way; in the five months they had owned Sinister, Neal had never recovered from the shock of hearing her purr and whine when she talked to or about the bird.

It was hard for Margaret, of course. She was forty now. She had never been able to carry a baby. She had made four tries before her gynecologist discouraged the idea of her ever having children.

Both Neal and Margaret had been disheartened by it. But it was worse for a woman. Neal supposed that was why she kept herself so busy with all her projects and why she fussed so about her figure. You couldn't blame her for being self-absorbed. Unlike Neal, she received no gratification of the sort he found in his work, in helping people. Gardening and cooking and keeping house could be stretched just so far . . . So Margaret studied languages and measured herself and fawned over Sinister, and read books on astrology and the occult.

Neal said, "Is he at Dr. Halliday's?"

"Yes. Him knew, too. Him trembled all the way over there."

"He'll be all right."

"You didn't even notice him was gone."

"I'm sorry, dear."

Back to her normal tone then. "Neal, how's that little girl whose brother you helped?"

"Penny Bissel? I suppose she's fine."

"Do you ever see her?"

"She drops in from time to time. In fact, I think she's coming by the clinic tomorrow . . . What made you think of her?"

"I spoke to him the other day in town."

"Forrest?"

"Is that his first name? I was in Piermont. He passed me on the street."

"He knew who you were?"

"Oh, yes. He gave me a very nice hello."

"Forrest Bissell said hello to you?"

"Yes . . . And he asked how you were."

"I see . . . Strange."

"He's a Scorpio."

"*What?*"

"He's a Scorpio."

"Margaret, you're not making any sense!"

She did that same thing again with her eyes, closing them and then opening them. "What are you yelling at me for, Neal?"

"I'm sorry . . . I just don't understand."

"He was born October twenty-seventh, that's all. Which makes him a Scorpio."

"Margaret, how would you know when Forrest Bissel was born?"

"You're overreacting, Neal."

"Well, did you have a long conversation with him or what?"

"I do believe you're jealous."

"Margaret, he is *not* a very reliable character, that's all. He has no business starting conversations with you!"

She smiled. "He didn't start a conversation, Neal. I overheard him telling some man that he was saving his money to go to Europe: that he was going to leave on his birthday, October twenty-seventh . . . that's all."

Neal didn't say anything. His heart was beating fast.

Margaret said, "I wish you liked astrology better."

"Why?"

"Because one day I might surprise you."

But he was not listening to her now. He was thinking that if a part of him did want a showdown, a much larger part didn't, because for a moment in their conversation he had imagined they were on their way to one, and instantly he had told himself to deny everything, and then end things with Penny Bissel for once and for all.

He should do that anyway.

He told himself so while he was upstairs in his study, sorting through the material for the book.

Yes, ideally an enthusiastic and pretty young girl should be there to have the nightcaps with him and tell him he was going to be famous, and then make love with him for a long time. But that was fantasy-land, like those science-fiction stories Margaret enjoyed, in which a man would take the elevator in his apartment building to the wrong floor and find himself entering a new life with his name on the door of another apartment and another wife and family waiting for him, or a man would wake up with a different face, a new nationality, everything about his life changed.

Neal knew well from his years at Rock-Or that there were many neurotics who could not be happy except in the anticipation of change. The change itself meant nothing to such people; when they would make it, the next wish would be to change again.

Why was he even entertaining these ideas?

He was like some schoolboy enlarging on a fantasy until reality was forced out of proportion.

The more he saw of Penny Bissel, the more he was indulging the fantasy and letting go of reality.

Yet as he sat at his desk looking out at the moonlight on the river, he heard reality beneath him, and it made him wince with displeasure.

"*Dove c'è qui un buon ristorante?*" the voice on the record said.

"Where is there a good restaurant?"

*"Dove c'è qui un buon ristorante?"*

*"Non c'è nessuno che parli inglese?"*

"Is there anyone who speaks English?"

*"Non c'è nessuno che parli inglese?"*

He had a sudden vision of Penny running toward him in the field that day they had driven up to Bear Mountain, how they had run toward each other through the tall elephant grass, and the scent of the sun in her hair when he caught her to him and her fingers held on to his shirt, both of them laughing so hard.

*"Avanti!"*

"Come in!"

*"Avanti!"*

Once, in his office, she had said to him, in the middle of some idiotic diatribe he had been making about Forrest's unconscious wish to be punished as his father had beaten him when he was a child, "Neal? How long will it be before you'll touch me?"

He had kissed her that day for the first time, near-to-crazy at the way it made him feel, hardly able to stop, or to care that someone could happen into his office and find them like that.

She had said afterward, "I knew, Neal."

"What?"

"How it would be with us. That it would be like this."

Remember? She was wearing a long-sleeved white wool dress with a pin made from a penny on the collar.

She had pennies on everything, her handkerchiefs and sweaters and even one on the door of her father's car. Neal had bought her a coffee mug in New City with a penny on it.

*"Un uovo alla cocca."*

"A boiled egg."

*"Un uovo alla cocca."*

Tomorrow, he'd take her to the '76 House in Old Tappan for lunch.

CHAPTER 3

Wednesday night.

Archie's glasses were lost. While they searched the apartment for them, the phone rang.

Archie said to Dru, "I'll get it. May I tell whoever's calling that we're on our way out?"

"Why ask me?"

"Because it'll be for you," he said. "It always is."

"Archie, don't act so put-upon. I didn't lose your glasses, you lost them."

But the call was not for Dru; it was Archie's father.

"How are you?" Archie said without much enthusiasm.

His father said, "If I felt any better I'd be in jail for rape."

Archie made an effort to laugh. Years ago, when Archie had been in analysis, his father's perpetual braggadocio on the subject of his sexual prowess had frequently tied Archie's stomach in knots. Most of his fifty-minute hours had been spent reliving the anxieties he had felt as the young son of a self-proclaimed Don Juan.

Now Archie was more bored than anything else by it, and still resentful at what it had done to his mother. After the divorce, she had never remarried, and she had gone to her

20

grave pretending to everyone, including Archie, that the stories of Frank Gamble's infidelities were exaggerated. They weren't, but she imagined her word was accepted. It was a way of saving face. When Archie was a boy he used to hear her tell his father: "I know you're seeing other women, but don't flaunt it. Don't embarrass me before my friends."

While Archie talked to his father, he studied his reflection in the Constitution mirror above the telephone stand. He remembered when he used to find gray hairs among the coal-black ones on his head; now the reverse was true. At forty-two, could he still claim he was prematurely gray? He decided that his friends who weren't gray probably darkened their hair.

". . . had a visitor today," his father was saying. "Female, naturally, but a very special female."

"Good for you. Look, Dad, Dru and I are on our way to the country. Did you call about something in particular?"

"Don't you want to know who my female friend was?" he said.

"Who?"

"Guess."

"Come on, Dad. I don't have time."

"Liddy."

Archie reached in the pocket of his blazer for a cigarette. "Oh?"

"Is that all you have to say? Oh?"

"How is she?" He found a match and lit the cigarette.

"She's the same Liddy. I'll never know how you let that slip through your fingers."

Archie's father wasn't fond of Dru. She wouldn't flirt back with him the way Liddy would.

Archie said, "Is she planning to stay in New York?" Dru came out of the bedroom carrying his glasses. She walked across and Archie bent down so she could put them on him.

"Oh, yes. She has an apartment on East Fifty-Seventh Street."

"Alone?"

"Well, as alone as a woman like Liddy will ever be."

"Good for her."

"She asked about you."

"Uh huh."

"Wanted to know if you were happy."

"Ummm."

"I said you might not be happy, but you were cheerful."

"You have a lot of insight," Archie said dryly.

"Are you going to see her, son?"

He was never able to adjust to his father's calling him "son." It invariably embarrassed him.

He said, "What for?"

"What *for?* You were married to her for fifteen years!"

"So?"

"I thought you'd want to see her. I thought I was bringing you good news. She wants to see *you.* She says it's important. Urgent."

Dru sat across the room from him turning the pages of *Life.* Normally she would be making frantic motions for him to get off the phone, but she sensed that the conversation was about Liddy. She was wearing her best I-Won't-Make-A-Scene expression, which usually indicated that she would, delayed-reaction style, three hours from now or three days from now. Suddenly. Zap!

Archie said, "Dad, we're going to be late if we don't leave right away."

"Where are you going in the country?"

"I have some research to do for this astrology show."

"What a lot of bunk that is. Astrology."

"Yeah. Right."

Why did Archie remember then an afternoon when his father had come into his bedroom—what was Archie, ten, eleven? His father had picked up the journal Archie was writing in, and read aloud the quotation Archie was copying from

F. Scott Fitzgerald. *"In a real dark night of the soul, it is always three o'clock in the morning."*

His father had bent double laughing until tears rolled down his cheeks. He had tugged on Archie's hair and guffawed. "What bunk! And what do you know about dark nights of the soul, Little Lord Fauntleroy? You're as self-pitying as your mother is!"

Archie had actually struck him, and his father had stood there with a look of stunned hatred on his face, his hand holding the spot near his nose where Archie's blow had landed.

His father had said, "If I hit girls, I'd hit you back."

Now his father said, "I don't know what Liddy wants, but it's urgent. That I do know. Call her, son. Here's her private number."

"I don't need it, thanks."

"You ought to call her, you know."

"Sometime I will."

Dru had read about a restaurant in Old Tappan called '76 House. It dated back to the eighteenth century, with lots of old wood, supposedly, and heavy on atmosphere. The plan was to have dinner there, then proceed to Grandview-on-Hudson. Mrs. Dana had invited them for nine-thirty, warning Dru that the hill was long and treacherous and that you had to drive along River Road slowly or you'd miss the right turn which led up to the house.

As Archie drove the Triumph across the George Washington bridge, he asked Dru again, "Why doesn't she want to tell him about it ahead of time?"

Dru had the Goodavage book on her lap; she was paging through it.

She said, "What do you think your reaction would have been four months ago, if I had told you your astro-twin was dropping in?"

"I'd have had you committed."

"Soooo. She's not telling him ahead of time."

"What a pleasant surprise he's in for."

"She says it's the best way."

"I wouldn't blame him if he slugged me," Archie said.

"He won't. He's a psychologist."

"What's that got to do with it?"

"I just think a psychologist would have more control."

"Did you ever hear the old saying, 'Physician, heal thyself'?"

"He's not a doctor, Archie. He's a Ph.D."

"I hope this place has a steak."

"Is that what you feel like? Again?"

"I like steak."

"He does, too. Neal Dana. Margaret said he could eat steak every night of his life."

Archie groaned. "You two have compared notes already?"

"We had a little talk."

"Why didn't you say so? You said you just called her for directions."

Dru said, "We didn't talk long. I told you he was writing a book."

"Ummm. If you want to use that basis for comparison, every other joker in the country is living a life parallel to mine."

"I'm not trying to talk you into anything, Archie. I'm not Mrs. Muckermann."

"What else did she say about him?"

"Let's see. He's nearsighted and he always misplaces his glasses, and he attended the Journalism School at the University of Missouri, and he was in psychoanalysis for four years, and—"

"Okay, okay."

"Archie?"

"What?"

"Listen to this." She picked up the Goodavage book and read to him:

*". . . George A. Blunden, Jr., and Douglas Fillebrown, who were both born in the same year, month, date, hour, and close to the same minute in the same state (Portsmouth and Gorham, N.H., on November thirteenth, 1944). On June twenty-second, 1964, a fire broke out in a three-story Phi Kappa Alpha fraternity house at the University of New Hampshire. A dozen young men scrambled to safety—but not George Blunden nor Douglas Fillebrown. Inexplicably, both burned to death at the same time. Was this predestined? Could it have been predicted or prevented? What science other than astrology can explain why these 'astro-twins' were attracted to the same university? Why did they choose the same fraternity? Why did they have to be in the same fraternity house at the exact time it burned down? Why were they the only ones who didn't escape?"*

She put the book down. "Are you *ready* for that?"

Archie laughed. "Coincidence."

"You want to hear some more *coincidences?*"

"Ummm hmmm." But he wasn't paying attention now. Mercury and Saturn were stimulating that opposition full force, for he was distracted again, and by thoughts of Liddy again.

What could be so important that made her eager to see him, and why hadn't she given his father some idea what it was about? His father and Liddy had always been very close. It used to annoy Archie that she called his father "Frank" and treated him like her favorite confidant. Toward the end of their marriage, Archie had even imagined that Liddy told his father about her affairs, that the two of them discussed it over drinks—those long drinking sessions they put in together—and that they laughed at him behind his back.

Would Liddy do that to him?

He was still unconvinced that she wouldn't, even though she had wept (unusual for Liddy) when he had accused her of it, and asked him how in God's name he could think that of her; wasn't there any feeling for her left from what they had had?

The trouble was, there was too much feeling left then; maybe there still was.

She had come back to New York alone. He received no small satisfaction from that news. He was sure that Moneybags had left her, for married to him, Liddy could have everything, all that money could buy and all the affairs she wanted. Moneybags was one of those strange men who not only didn't demand fidelity from his wife, but felt perversely pleased with the idea other men could love her although she belonged to him. Archie had only a hazy memory of Moneybags, though he had met him four or five times. He was the type who wore dark glasses at night.

"The second 'astro-twin' was found lying dead on the floor," Dru continued. "Autopsies revealed that marzey doats and dozey doats and little lambsy divy. Isn't that fascinating, Archie?"

Archie said, "Is it documented? Dates, places?"

"Oh my, yes. The mares came from Sioux City, Iowa."

"That's interesting."

She slammed the book shut.

"Something the matter?" Archie asked her.

"What could be the matter?"

"I don't know. The way you slammed the book. I thought something was the matter."

"You're just oversensitive."

He turned right at the end of the bridge, fed fifty cents to the toll booth, and swung onto Palisades Parkway.

"These brakes aren't any too good," he said. "Why don't you take this car in for a complete checkup?"

Dru didn't answer him. She was looking out the window at the river.

C H A P T E R  4

"Like it?" Margaret asked.

It was eight-twenty P.M.

She was fastening a gold pin to her yellow cotton dress. The face of the pin bore the figure of a female carrying an ear of corn.

Neal Dana said, "It's very attractive . . . Margaret, you're going to be late for your class."

Usually Margaret left the house on the dot of eight. Her Italian class at the New School in Manhattan began at nine-thirty. The day before, Neal had told Penny to come at nine.

Margaret combed her hair before the Constitution mirror in their bedroom. "Do you know what the pin means, Neal?"

"No. You really are going to be late."

"It's the virgin for Virgo, my sun sign."

"Very attractive." He checked the time on the clock-radio with his wristwatch. Eight-twenty-one.

Margaret said, "There've been a lot of famous Virgos. Greta Garbo's one, Sophia Loren's one, Arthur Godfrey, Leonard Bernstein, Tolstoy was one, Theodore Dreiser—"

Neal interrupted her. "Wouldn't every sign have its share of famous people?"

27

"Neal, what's the matter with you tonight?" She put down her comb and turned to look at him. "You're so impatient."

"Something's the matter with you, if you ask me. You're never late for class, Margaret. Tonight you're just unconcerned . . . I don't know. It isn't like you."

She smiled. "No, I suppose it isn't. Virgos are usually fairly consistent. But you know, Neal, Virgo is ruled by Mercury, too, as Gemini is, so I have my 'mercurial' moments."

Neal said, "I'll turn on the outside lights for you," and started from the room.

"Wait a minute, Neal."

"Honey, it's almost eight-*thirty*." He forced a pained little smile.

"Never mind the time. May I ask you something?"

She waited for him to respond. It was a mannerism Neal had catalogued in his study of everyday behavior: that of people introducing their remarks with "May I ask you something?" Most people who had this habit were afraid of being aggressive, or *were* aggressive and fearful of showing it. It was a repetition of an adolescent situation: children were often not permitted to ask questions or assert themselves. They needed permission and encouragement.

In Margaret's case it sprang from her wish to camouflage her aggressive nature. It was almost patronizing, for both Margaret and Neal knew that neither hell nor high water could keep her from posing the question she had in mind.

Neal said, "What do you want to know?"

Eight-twenty-five. *Jesus!*

"Stop worrying about the time. You keep looking at your watch."

"What do you want to ask me?"

"Why you have such a block against astrology," she said.

"It's not particular to astrology. I have the same reaction to phrenology, numerology, palmistry, fortune-telling by tea leaves, and all the various arts of divination."

"Dear, astrology isn't in the same category."

"All right, Margaret. It isn't."

"It *isn't*. Neal, President Franklin D. Roosevelt was interested in astrology. Did you know that?"

"No. He was probably interested in a lot of things I'm not interested in."

Margaret sat down on the edge of the bed.

*Sat down!* At eight-twenty-six!

"You see, FDR was well aware of this pattern made by the conjunction of Jupiter and Saturn every twenty years," said Margaret, "which seems to coincide with the death of American presidents every twenty years."

"Oh, *Margaret*."

"Neal, don't scoff. *Please*." She folded her arms across her breasts and regarded him with that didactic expression, which usually preceded a stretch of sermonizing.

"You don't have to convince *me*," Neal put in. "There's probably something to it."

He realized the futility of any attempt to keep her from continuing.

Let her get it over with.

He also folded his arms, in such a way that he could see his watch, and waited for her to have her say.

"William Henry Harrison was elected in 1840," said she, "and died in office. In 1860 there was Lincoln. In 1880 there was Garfield. In 1900 there was McKinley; 1920, Harding; 1940, Roosevelt. And then Kennedy in 1960 . . . Neal, don't you find it an extraordinary coincidence?"

"Yes, yes, I admit that it is," he said.

"They *all* died in office."

"So they did. I wasn't aware of it."

What was *wrong* with Margaret tonight? She was finished dressing, was ready to go—why didn't she go?

She said, "Harrison, Lincoln, McKinley and Roosevelt were

all Aquarians. Garfield and Harding were Scorpians. And Kennedy was a Gemini."

Neal said nothing; he shifted his weight from one foot to the other.

Margaret said, "Doesn't any of it interest you, dear?"

"Not really. I'm sorry."

Then she said, "I'm not going to my Italian class tonight, Neal."

"You're *not?*"

"Darling, don't look so shocked."

Eight-thirty! If he phoned Penny now, right now, he could probably catch her before she left the house. But phone her from where?

He said, "How come?" His voice gave no indication of the panic loosed inside him.

"That's my little surprise."

"What is?"

"The reason I'm not going to my Italian class." She smiled at him coyly.

He had no time to fathom a possible reason for her missing school; he had to get out of there, immediately, get to a phone.

Margaret said, "I want you to promise me something, Neal."

"What?"

"That you'll be nice about my surprise . . . that you'll try to appreciate the fact I mean well."

A nervous burst of laughter broke from him. "I'll not only appreciate it, whatever it is, I'll get us something to celebrate it. How about that, Margaret? Just for tonight don't worry about wasting calories. Let me run into Piermont and get some champagne for us!"

"Now, Neal—"

"I mean it, darling! We never really celebrated my afternoon at Doubleday! And we haven't had champagne in a hell of a long time! Remember how we used to love to kill a few bottles of Piper in the evening? It'd be just the thing!"

He could drive down to the bottom of the hill, park the

car, explain to the Nickersons there was something wrong with his phone, call Penny and tell her not to come. Then on to Piermont for the champagne.

"Maybe champagne will put you in a better mood for my surprise," said Margaret.

"Of course it will! It'll put us both in a good mood!"

"But let's call for a delivery, Neal."

"I need cigarettes, too . . . and I'd like to pick up something to go with the champagne. Maybe some good caviar, honey. Would you like that?"

She laughed. "All right. I haven't seen you this excited in a long time! . . . Neal?"

"What?"

"Don't drive too fast, darling."

What had ever made him ask Penny to come to the house in the first place? He supposed the reason was because he had so often envisioned her there with him. It was such a romantic house, wasn't it? From almost every window there was a view of the Hudson, and the green lights of the Tappan Zee bridge, the silhouettes of pines and evergreens, and the fireflies flickering in the darkness. The quiet, too, and the scent from the woods of foliage and dew wetting the earth. All the things he used to love to observe with Margaret, that they didn't notice together any more.

And the truth was he always thought of it as his house. He had been the one to find it and fall in love with it. Margaret had disliked the isolation. He had built the swimming pool and the upper porch to make Margaret happier there. When he had put the beams in the living-room ceiling he had gone to great trouble to find old wood which would match the original lumber: he had sweat out innumerable Saturday afternoons at auctions of old houses.

"Why?" Margaret wanted to know. "Will we always live here?"

"I'd like to."

"Not after the baby comes. It's too small."

The only good thing about their never having a baby was that they didn't need the "extra room." Margaret usually got her way, but about selling the house, Neal was adamant: not unless they had to.

Once Penny had said, "I'd love to see where you live. I'd like to be able to picture you in your surroundings, nights when I miss you so, Neal."

She had finally persuaded him. He'd never try it again, though.

He promised himself that as he rounded the curve of the drive and looked for a spot where he could park at the bottom of the hill.

After he called Penny, he would call Margaret, too, on some pretense. Did she have enough cigarettes? How about some fresh strawberries to put in the champagne glasses? Flimsy excuses, it was true, but there was no time to scheme, and he could not chance Minnie Nickerson's mentioning to Margaret that he had stopped by to telephone. It couldn't come as news to Margaret; she would suspect something immediately.

For the same reason, it was better not to say his phone was out of order. The strawberries were perfect! If she wanted strawberries, he'd have to go into Nyack. Anyone would appreciate his reluctance to drive all the way back up the hill just to learn if he should go to Piermont or Nyack. Minnie was a scatterbrain anyway, one of those vague animal-lovers who seldom concerned herself with the complexities of people. She was a half-deaf old maid with a bedridden mother to care for, and no friends. She minded her own business. Neal had always been grateful that she was the nearest neighbor.

He parked the car on the road near her house.

Eight-thirty-five!

If Penny had left, he would simply have to wait for her car, and invent some excuse explaining the delay to Margaret.

He cut across Minnie Nickerson's lawn, the wet grass soaking the cuffs of his trousers.

Then he heard the Doberman's angry barking, saw the dog heading for him, and saw the tree he would have to climb to keep from being torn apart.

Nine-two.

He crouched on the tree limb and watched helplessly while Penny drove the Ford Falcon up the hill.

"Minnie! Mrs. Nickerson!" His anguished cries were futile, as they had been when he had tried to make Penny hear him while she approached the turn. Every time he opened his mouth, the Doberman opened hers. He was treed like a cat.

Margaret would know everything the minute she saw Penny. Even if he were able to dream up some sort of reason for Penny's arrival at the house, on the very night Margaret had her class, there was no way he could predict what words the two of them would exchange.

He was trapped.

The funny thing was, it was Margaret he was most worried about now. As controlled, as consistent and steady as she was, there had been that period three years ago when she had gone to pieces. There had been no infidelity involved, but she had seemed obsessed with the idea Neal didn't want her, that he would like a divorce. It was understandable. The doctor had just told Margaret she should abandon the idea of having children.

"I'm not good for anything," was the remark she made most often during that time.

Then she had gone to Bucks County to stay with her mother. It had taken Neal six months to talk her into returning.

Remember those six months?

They were the most wretched months of his life. My God how he had missed Margaret!

What kind of convenient amnesia had overtaken him that he could forget that?

He sat there in the tree, suddenly unable to remember Penny Bissel's face.

Then he saw Minnie Nickerson's porch light turn on.

"Kendal? Kendal?" she called.

The dog gave a whine and danced nervously around the tree.

"Kendal! Come on, girl! Come!"

The dog barked, moved away from the tree, then came back.

Minnie Nickerson clapped her hands. "Hurry, Kendal! Hurry!"

Now the dog began to lope across the lawn. He stopped once, looked back at the tree, and then obediently continued toward her mistress.

Neal Dana slid down the tree trunk. When his feet touched ground, he ran.

Margaret's voice, shrill, from the upstairs landing.

". . . stupid! Deceiving yourself this way, humiliating yourself this way, without any semblance of character or integrity; cheap, CHEAP!"

"Shut up! You shut up!" Penny was up there with her.

As Neal crossed the living room, running, shouting Margaret's name, he heard her scream, "No, I won't shut up! Face what you are—cheap, CHE—"

Then the lightning crack of flesh being slapped, followed by the thunderous sound of someone falling backward, down the stairs.

It was Margaret's body that bounced and rolled toward Neal, Margaret's head that hit the marble-topped bench on the landing, and her blood on Neal Dana's hands, soaking into his shirt as he gathered her to him.

Her eyes were open, staring into his, as lusterless as the eyes of a fish on the end of a hook.

CHAPTER 5

'76 House had all the charm of an old Colonial inn. It was conducive to drinking, crowded, and the service was slow. Archie and Dru polished off three martinis apiece before dinner, instead of the usual two apiece.

"I've been thinking about what I'll write when I finish this show," Archie said after they were served their filet mignons. "Maybe nonfiction for a change."

"As distinguished from the fiction of astrology."

"Yeah. Right."

"Like what?"

"Maybe that thing I've always wanted to do on symbiotic relationships."

"This meat doesn't have much flavor. I'm sorry," Dru said.

"It's not your fault. Filet mignon never does."

"You had your heart set on a nice juicy steak, too."

"Do you remember my idea for the study of symbiotic relationships, honey?"

She glanced meekly at him. "I don't even remember what symbiotic means."

"Symbiosis," said Archie, "literally means the living together of two dissimilar organisms when their association is mutually beneficial. But what I'm interested in is two people collaborating—people who can't do whatever it is they do for a living alone."

"Then why don't you just say collaborating? Why do you have to drag in this symbiotic business?"

Archie intoned, "And in accepting this Pulitzer, I must mention my wife's unquestioning support, her patience in listening to my ideas, and her remarkable attention span."

"Thank you, gentlemen of the press, I'd like to mention my husband's paranoia," said Dru, buttering a roll.

"Plain old collaboration is an oversimplification," Archie said. "I've collaborated a few times myself. But it isn't my way of life. I'm talking about people like Laurel and Hardy, Gilbert and Sullivan, the two men who write under the name Ellery Queen. People like that."

"Lerner and Loewe."

"Right. Rodgers and Hammerstein, Abbott and Costello—"

"You could even include criminals: Loeb and Leopold."

"Or spies," Archie said, "Burgess and Maclean."

"Explorers: Lewis and Clark."

"I'd call it *Two by Two*. That's a good title."

Dru said, "How about Simon and Garfunkel?"

"They're good. You see, it'd be interesting to discover why it is some people need to be teamed up to succeed."

"I love the title, Archie."

"Thanks, love. And what their personal relationships are like. Gilbert and Sullivan disliked each other intensely—they never socialized."

"How about Huntley and Brinkley?"

"Yes, and Sid Caesar and Imogene Coca—they never really came back after they split up."

"Jeanette MacDonald and Nelson Eddy," said Dru. She sang softly, " 'Rosemarie—I love you. I'm always thinking of you.' "

Archie said, "Husband and wife teams: Lunt and Fontanne,

the Durants, those mystery writers—what are their names? The Gordons."

"Elizabeth Taylor and Richard Burton," said Dru, "Archie and Liddy Gamble."

Archie put down his fork and leaned on his elbows. "All right, love, blow your cool and get it over with."

"I'm not going to blow my cool," she said. "Eat!"

"That last martini quenched my appetite."

"Well, I said the secret password. What's my prize?"

"Why can't you just let things drop?" said Archie.

"Why can't she? She called Father Gamble, didn't she?"

"You make him sound like a priest. I wis. you'd stop calling him *Father* Gamble."

Dru said, "In my family that's what we call fathers-in-law."

"Dad doesn't like it, either," said Archie.

"He just can't stand to be reminded of his age. The only reason I'd like to have a baby is to make him a grandfather." Dru stopped eating, too, and took out a cigarette.

Archie lit it for her. "What's the time?"

"We've got time. I asked you a question, Archie."

"It's eight o'clock. We've got to get from here to Grandview in an hour and a half, and I don't know the roads."

"She called him, didn't she?"

"Do you think she'd come back to New York and not call him? Liddy always liked Dad better than she liked me."

"Aw. Poor Archie."

"Knock it off, Dru. Okay?"

"Why should I?" she said.

The fight was on.

At a quarter to nine, Archie stopped outside Nyack so Dru could call Margaret Dana from a gasoline station pay phone.

"It's all right if we're late," she said, getting back in the car. "It seems he's gone out to buy some champagne."

"Some 'astro-twin,'" said Archie. "It's the last thing I'd do if I were in his shoes."

"No, Archie—he doesn't know yet. He just knows he's in for a surprise."

"Why the champagne?"

"*Some* men are big spenders."

Archie turned onto the highway. "That isn't why I didn't want you to have a brandy."

"Then why say 'the bill's already over twenty-five dollars'? That's what you said."

Archie put his hand on her knee. "Because I'm chicken. I just didn't want the argument to have any more fuel."

She put her hand over his. "I'm sorry, Archie."

"Let's forget it."

"Am I a bitch?"

"Huh uh."

"She wouldn't have blown her cool like that, would she?"

Archie said, "The hell with what Liddy would do or wouldn't do."

"Do you mean that?"

"I mean that."

She let go of his hand and leaned back against the seat. "It's nice in the country, isn't it? I wish we could afford a place out here."

"I was thinking the same thing," Archie said. "Maybe for the summer. Maybe the Danas might know of something for rent."

"I'd love it!"

"It'd be good to get away from New York."

Nyack was a tacky town. They both commented on it as they drove through, and Dru spoke of Sneden's Landing, a nearby community supposedly filled with artists and writers and theater people.

"But that's just what I'd like to get away from," said Archie.

"Okay, love, we're on Piermont Avenue now. This is supposed to turn into River Road, so keep your eyes peeled."

"I wouldn't like to live right next door to the Joneses, though, Arch."

"How the hell are we different from the Joneses?" he said.

"We are, that's all. You'll never admit that. It's reverse snobbery on your part."

"I said, *how* are we different?"

"For one thing, we don't have children."

"That's about the seventh time you've mentioned not having children tonight. I think you want them."

"Them?" she said. "I don't even want *one*."

"How else are we different?"

"Oh, Archie, come off it!"

"You mean the fact we smoke opium and have orgies?"

"You don't go to work every day."

"No. When I go into my study I look at dirty pictures for six hours."

"You know what I mean. You're creative."

"That's why I'm on my way to see my 'astro-twin,' " Archie said, "because I'm creative. It hasn't got anything to do with commercialism."

"I *don't* believe you. Tear you down, you'll build yourself up. Build you up, you'll tear yourself down."

"There ought to be an in-between."

"We're on River Road, Arch."

"Fine . . . Anyway, I don't learn anything from living with artists and writers and theater people. We're all too neurotic. No one wants to buy a book about neurotics."

Dru rolled the window down and tossed away her cigarette. "You're right. The best sellers are about normal people. *The Exhibitionist, Myra Beckenridge . . .*"

When they reached the turn, Archie slowed down. "I think this is it."

"Archie, she said it'd be on the left."

"We're not coming from Piermont. We're approaching it from the other direction, so it's this right turn."

"She said it was a very long hill. This doesn't look like it leads up a long hill."

"It does, though—there's the sign."

"Where?"

"Near that Ford Consul. See?"

"Oh, Archie, remember our Consul?"

He made the turn. "I remember mine. It wasn't ours. You wouldn't marry me yet."

"I thought you were an alcoholic. You drank an awful lot in those days."

"Some hill! Jesus!"

"Be careful, Arch . . . Archie?"

"What?"

"Don't have too much champagne, promise?"

"Oh, am I glad I reminded you of the old days!"

"We've got to come back down this hill, that's all. And I know how you love champagne."

"And Scotch, and gin, and vodka, and rum, and brandy."

"But champagne more. You never think it's affecting you until too late."

"I'll be good."

"I don't *believe* this hill! Are you *ready* for this hill?"

When they reached the top, Archie parked the Triumph under a tree beside a Ford Falcon. Next to it was a beige Volkswagen.

There were no outside lights; even the porch light was not on.

Dru said, "Thanks *a lot* for this enthusiastic reception. I can hardly hear anything over the noise of the brass band."

"Maybe we're in the wrong place." He squashed his cigarette in the ashtray and looked over his shoulder at the house again. "Nobody seems to be running out to greet us."

"Why don't you go see if the Danas live here, darling? I'll wait."

Archie got out and walked across the gravel drive to the house. There was a screened-in porch at the front and Archie knocked on the door. No one came.

He tried the screen door—it was open—and went across the porch and tapped the brass knocker on the door to the house.

A few minutes passed before a man answered. He looked like a younger Joe DiMaggio, as tall as Archie was but with a receding hairline and a thinner build. Brown eyes, unsmiling.

What was the noise in the background?

"I must have the wrong house," Archie apologized. "I'm looking for the Danas'."

"This is the Danas'."

The noise came from the upstairs of the house, a muffled sound.

"Is Mrs. Dana here? I'm Archie Gamble from New York."

"She's not here." He didn't have the door open very wide. He had the suspicious attitude of someone who was on guard for theft or a mugging.

"She was expecting me," Archie said, and before he could add anything about Dru's phone call to Margaret Dana less than thirty minutes ago, the man interrupted him.

"We weren't expecting anyone. Mrs. Dana isn't here."

Then Archie knew what that sound was: it was a woman crying. Trying not to make noise—perhaps crying into a pillow, but crying audibly, nevertheless.

Archie decided not to pursue it. Whatever the situation had been thirty minutes ago, it was changed now; it was obvious Dru and he were unwelcome.

"I'm sorry I disturbed you," Archie said, "but Mrs. Dana invited—"

"She isn't here," Dana repeated emphatically.

And Archie gave him a quick salute. "Thanks for the trouble."

The door was shut in his face.

"If you want my opinion," Archie said as he started the car, "she sprung the surprise on him and they had a fight about it."

"I don't *believe* her!" said Dru. "She'd let us come all the way out here, and not even show her face!"

"Her makeup's running, from the sound of things."

"But Arch, over the phone she sounded so convinced everything would go smoothly. She said he was out buying champagne and he was in a very festive mood."

Archie turned down the hill. "I have nothing but respect for him. I'm glad he's my 'astro-twin.' If you'd pulled this on me without any warning, I'd be tempted to give you a good clout in the mouth, too."

"He hit her?"

"How would I know? I didn't see her."

"You said 'too.' You'd be tempted to give me a good clout in the mouth, too."

Archie said, "I don't know what he did. I only know she's upstairs crying."

"He's buying champagne one minute and chickening out the next. That sounds like you, all right. He probably wants it all to himself."

"In between minutes the poor guy learned his wife turned him in as an 'astro-twin' for a network TV show." Archie laughed. "I was about as welcome as the man in the white coat who drives the wagon from the funny farm."

"Moody!" Dru said. "He didn't have to take it out on us!"

"I don't think he did. I think he took it out on her."

"Poor woman."

"Oh, come on, Dru!" Archie said. "She must be some kind of a nut. Who'd bother with this stuff?"

"Maybe they need the money."

"Three hundred and fifty dollars? She knew that was all there was in it for him. Scale."

"You're beautiful," Dru said. "One minute you tell me we're no different from the Joneses, and the next minute you talk as though three hundred and fifty dollars wasn't a lot of money to the average person."

Archie said, "It's a lot of money to me, too. But not enough to make me go on CBS as an 'astro-twin.'"

"If he'd have cooperated, you'd have had to go on."

"Would you believe ten thousand three hundred and fifty dollars?"

"Archie," she said, "what's the matter with you? Why are we going so—"

The windshield was shattered by the impact as the car slammed into the tree.

"Dru, are you all right?"

"I think so."

"Get out!"

The radiator was smoking.

"I can't," she said.

"Here, on my side." He held out his hand and pulled her toward him.

"Are *you* all right, darling?" she said.

"Yes."

"God, my God, I thought we were done for, Arch!"

"The brakes just gave out."

"Thank God for that tree," Dru said. "We could have landed right in the river."

"Let me get the flashlight."

"Don't, Arch, it looks like it's going to blow up."

"It's all right." He leaned inside and opened the glove compartment.

"Oh, Archie, our car! Look at our car!"

"Don't be so commercial," he said. "Be creative. What do we do now?"

"We go back up and use their phone."

"No. We go down to the road and thumb a ride to a gas station."

"Archie," she said, "it's their hill! They're responsible!"

"Because we haven't had our brakes checked in the last six months?"

"I'm going up there and use their phone!"

"Dru, we'll hail a car and ask the driver for a ride to the nearest gas station."

She said, "We can't just leave the car. Anyone going up or down this hill could be killed, Archie."

"Then we'll hail a car and ask the driver to report the trouble to the nearest gas station."

"They might not have a tow truck. He might say he'd do it and not do it. Oh, look, Archie," she said. "It's Margaret Dana's fault. You stay with the car, and let me go back and use their phone."

"I'll go with you."

"No! Somebody has to stay with the car . . . Honey, are you *sure* you're all right, Arch?"

"Yes. Are you sure *you* are?"

"I am, but you're all out of breath and upset."

"Dru, I'm not upset! Jesus! We almost got killed!"

"Give me the flashlight. You stay with the car."

"I'll come with you."

"I don't want you with me, Archie. If they've been fighting, it's best for a woman to go up there."

"What sense does that make?" he said.

"Because Margaret Dana and I have talked on the phone. So I know her a little."

"And my twin?"

"I'm a woman in distress, remember?" Dru said. "And if he's anything like you, bubby, I can handle him."

CHAPTER 6

One day Margaret had said, "Look, Neal, what I bought for us. Aren't they cute?"

"What are they?" One was pink and one was blue. They looked like pillows with attached handles.

"They're called Slumber Bags, dear. Fifteen ninety-nine apiece—I got them at Sears."

"But what are they, Margaret?"

"Sleeping bags! They're specially treated to repel water and mildew. They have cotton flannelette liners, and they're machine washable. Ideal for camping trips."

*Camping* trips.

When had they ever gone camping?

At the time, Neal had been reminded of a study he had read in one of his professional journals dealing with housewives' spending habits. It claimed that one of the reasons women bought so many utterly useless things, like bric-a-brac, or decorative wall shelves, or yard ornaments (or Vycron polyester sleeping bags?), was that they felt unloved and were forcing their husbands to buy them these "gifts" out of the household budget.

45

As Neal had predicted to himself, they had never found a use for the Slumber Bags.

Now, at least, there was a use for one of them.

Margaret's body was contained in the pink one.

So often Neal had asked the criminal patients he treated, who always swore they were innocent of the crimes for which they had been convicted, "But why did you run? Why didn't you face the police if you weren't guilty of anything? Only the guilty run."

Behind him in the bathtub, his bloodstained shirt and pants and socks were soaking in cold water.

Call the police? For what? To be told that a Doberman pinscher couldn't testify that Neal was treed while his "lover" arrived for an unexpected confrontation with his wife?

Penny had expected Neal to come out and greet her. She had combed her hair and fixed her makeup, finished her cigarette before getting out of the Falcon. She knew how hard it was to distract Neal if he were working; he had mentioned that he was trying to finish his outline. Finally, she had gone inside.

—Darling, I'm here! Where are you, Neal?

A bird whistled, a black parrot in a white cage on the living-room table.

—Hi, who are you, bird?

—I'm Sinister.

—You're Sinister? Har de har, har, har. You don't look Sinister. You look like a grouchy old parrot . . . Neal, are you upstairs, darling?

—I'm Sinister. I love the view.

—It's a nice view, you're right . . . Shall I come up, darling?

—"It came upon the mid-night clear, that glor-ri-ous song of old."

—It isn't Christmas yet, bird! Neal, are you in the john?

—"From Ang-gels bend-ing near the earth, To touch their harps of gold. Peace on earth, Goodwill to men!"

—Did you fall in or something, darling?

—*Dove c'è qui un buon ristorante?*

—Be quiet, bird! You talk too much!

—*Non c'è nessuno che parli inglese?*

As she went up the stairs, she said, —Am I too early, Neal?

—I suspect you're right on time.

They met like that at the top of the stairs.

—Mrs. Da-Da-Dana?

—Good evening.

—I . . . Good evening.

—Aren't you going to introduce yourself?

—Yes. I. Oh, cripes.

—Penny Bissel?

—Oh wow. Yes.

—How do you do?

—Cripes. I mean, all right, I'm caught red-handed.

—Neal's at the store. He should be back soon.

—I mean, there's no sense being polite about it. I'm sorry. I'm *sorry*, but Neal and I are in love.

—Pffft.

—What's that supposed to mean? That we're not in love?

—That's a very pretty dress you're wearing, Penny.

—Don't try to be nice to me like I'm nothing!

—What would you like me to do, dear?

—Give Neal a divorce.

—As he wishes.

—Well, he wishes you would. He would have had to tell you eventually anyway.

—Would you like some soda pop? I think we have some. I keep a supply of it for the neighborhood children who come up to use our pool.

—Listen, Mrs. Dana, Neal and I love each other very much!

—I think we have some chocolate Yoo-Hoo. Would you like a glass while you're waiting for Neal to return?

—It isn't fair for you to hold on to Neal!

—Or just plain Coke?

—You can't give him children! Neal would make a great father!

—Don't go too far, Miss Bissel.

—That hits home, doesn't it, *Mrs.* Dana?

—*D'accord.*

—*What?*

—I agreed with you.

—So don't treat me like a child, Mrs. Dana. I'm more of a woman than you are, or ever were!

—May I ask you something?

—Go ahead.

—How did you become so stupid! Deceiving yourself this way, humiliating yourself this way, without any semblance of character or integrity; cheap, CHEAP!

—Shut up! You shut up!

Then Neal's voice from downstairs. —Margaret? Margaret!

—No, I won't shut up! Face what you are—cheap, CHE—

And even if the police did believe that Neal had been treed or running up the hill through most of it, would they also believe that Margaret had fallen because she had jumped back after slapping Penny?

At best, wouldn't they imagine that Penny had pushed Margaret?

And since they were trained to suspect the worst, wouldn't they discard all those details and dream up a new version, starting with Neal as Margaret's murderer, Penny his accomplice?

"Neal?" Penny came into the bathroom, her long blond hair pushed behind her ears, her eyes swollen from crying. "The car went around the bend. There were two people in it, Neal. There was a woman with him."

"Get me a shirt from the top drawer in the bedroom on the right," he said. He was pulling on a pair of old khakis.

"Who *were* they, Neal?"

"I don't know. He said Margaret invited him. She was planning some kind of surprise. I don't know, and I don't have time to think about it now."

"Oh, cripes."

"Penny, get me that shirt!"


At least she had stopped crying. Stupidly, they had gotten into an argument, with Margaret's lifeless body between them, just before the stranger had knocked on the door.

—Didn't you see my car at the bottom of the hill?

—No, Neal. I didn't.

—Didn't you see the Volkswagen still in the yard. You know I don't drive a Volkswagen, yet you walked right in the house without giving it a thought!

—For all I knew she could have taken the bus to New York!

—The *bus!* The bus only goes to 138th Street! Why would she go on the bus when she has a car?

—I didn't think, Neal! I was too excited about seeing you, your house!

—Stop calling it *my* house. It was Margaret's house, too!

—Margaret! *Margaret!* You came in and called *her* name! You didn't call my name!

She had burst into noisy, quacking tears, crying the whole time the stranger was talking with Neal at the door. Neal had been forced to slap her face to make her quiet.

He had told her, "Now you listen to this: this is a whole other ballgame! Do you understand? *Murder.* Do you appreciate that?"

"I didn't touch her, Neal."

"I believe you. Who else do you think will, under the circumstances?"

"No one will."

"And no one's going to get a chance to disbelieve you. But you've got to pull yourself together, Pen. You've got to!"

She did.

Could she maintain it? Not just through the next few hours, but through the months ahead?

She appeared in the doorway with a white shirt in her hand.

"Not a white one!" he barked at her. "I'm not going out and dig in a white—"

Her face began to wither. "Dig," was all she could say, as though the fact he had to bury Margaret's body was just beginning to sink in.

"Pen," he said gently, "Oh, Pen, listen," holding her arms with his hands. "I know how you feel. I know I'm not helping any—shouting at you, losing my temper, but we've got to do this, Pen; we've got to save ourselves. It was a terrible accident, Pen, but it *was* an accident. Penny, the only sin we've committed is that we became involved. We didn't wish Margaret any harm."

She murmured something Neal couldn't hear.

"What did you say?" he asked.

"I said, would you have divorced Margaret for me?"

"Pen, listen. Listen! Pay attention to what's going on right now. We can't afford to think of anything else now. Do you see?"

"You wouldn't have," she said.

He had no choice but to hold her with firm hands and tell her emphatically, "Of course I would have! You know I would have!"

He would bury her in the woods in back of the house.

No one ever walked through them because of the snakes. There were rumors that there were rattlers as well as copperheads up there. Neal had posted signs on several trees surrounding the woods, warning people of the danger. Neighbors lectured their children about it, and when the man came to read the electric meter, which was placed on a post at the entrance to the woods, he made fast work of it, and wore high boots like the ones Neal was pushing his feet into now.

A rattler, a copperhead, was no more terrifying to Neal Dana than a common garter snake; any sort of snake was loathsome to him. He had tried to rid himself of this prejudice, this fear, ever since he was a small boy. A framed copy of a poem D. H. Lawrence had written hung above his desk at Rock-Or. "Snake." About a man who had killed a blacksnake and then regretted missing "my chance with one of the lords/ Of life." But no such noble sentiment moved him that night to face the possibility of an encounter with a reptile; he was moved by the rote reaction to save himself. Survival . . . the most basic human motivation.

He was aware of how close he was to losing his presence of mind and how carelessly he was provoking Penny into losing hers. While he waited for her to bring him another shirt, he took a deep breath, letting it out slowly, as though to prove to himself that he had hold, that he would be able to handle it now.

He didn't know how he was going to explain Margaret's disappearance, and he didn't try to estimate his chances of getting away with what he was doing; there was no time for any of that.

Penny brought him a blue work shirt. Neal put it on and headed for the basement to get the shovel.

When he reached the landing where Margaret had died, he heard the knock on the door.

"Just a minute!"

He turned around and went up the stairs.

"Pen? There's someone at the door." His voice was calm. She was standing by the bed. "I want you to stay here. Don't make a sound. I'll get rid of whoever it is."

She sat down on the bed and nodded her head affirmatively.

He smiled. He knew enough to say, "I love you, Pen."

She answered him with a weak tip of her lips.

Before he went downstairs, he closed the door of the bedroom containing the pink Vycron polyester Slumber Bag.

CHAPTER 7

"Don't you think you ought to call a service station before you come out?" Dru asked.

"Let me take a look." He held the screen door for her, waiting for her to follow him off the porch.

"But it isn't a simple wreck. We won't be able to drive away from it."

He didn't answer.

She sensed that he didn't want to let her inside the house.

"I'm sorry we're so much trouble."

He didn't answer. She walked alongside him in the bright moonlight. Archie was right; he did resemble Joe DiMaggio. But not the smiling baseball hero. He looked more like the DiMaggio whose pictures in the newspapers had worn such a melancholy expression after Marilyn Monroe's death.

"I know you weren't expecting us, but your wife—"

"You must have mistaken the date. She's not here."

"I didn't mistake the date."

"Well, she's not here."

Dru was tired of all the pretense. She said, "Your wife *must* have told you about us."

"What about you?"

52

"My husband isn't any more enthusiastic about astrology than you are. Neither am I. But Archie's not using a serious approach to the show. He's writing it sort of tongue-in-cheek."

He said, "I don't know anything about a show, Mrs. Gamble."

"Druscilla," she told him. No one she liked ever called her that, but she was feeling testy now, which always made her approach to things a little stilted. She was sure he knew all about the show and the reason she and Archie were there.

"I don't know anything about a show, *Druscilla*," he repeated.

"Well, my husband's writing a television special about astrology," she began, and then she went into all of it very quickly, winding up with her telephone call from the gas station to Margaret Dana. He walked along beside her with that same sad expression on his face, and when she was finished he didn't even comment.

So she said, "Not that it's any of my business, but in a way it is—because we drove all the way from New York to see you. It's a little odd that your wife would leave when she was expecting us."

"I see," was his answer.

"Oh, look, Mr. Dana—"

"Neal," he said.

"Neal . . . My husband said he wouldn't blame you if you gave Mrs. Dana a good clout in the mouth for pulling this on you. We understand."

He said nothing for a few seconds; then: "Is that your car up ahead?"

What else? It was on his hill, and Archie had set up the emergency flash signal lamp at the side.

Dru said, "No, I think that's a flying saucer. Didn't your wife tell you about that, either?"

"It wouldn't surprise me," he said, but there was no levity in his tone.

Poor Archie, a jack in one hand, a grease mark streaked across his nose, came stumbling forward with a big grin, the other hand outstretched, foolishly exclaiming, "We meet again."

Neal Dana established a world record for a brief handshake and said, "What happened?"

"My brakes *didn't* happen," said Archie.

Neal Dana was actually wiping the hand which had shaken Archie's on his trousers. "You won't be able to drive this car back to New York tonight," he said. "You can take our Volkswagen."

He produced a key ring from his pocket, unfastened it, and handed Archie one of the keys.

Archie said, "Look, how much would a taxi cost?"

"You'd have to wait a while for a taxi," said Neal Dana.

Money was not the object, from his point of view; getting rid of them as fast as possible was.

"Well, what did you expect him to do," Archie said as they turned off the West Side Highway at 19th Street, "ask us to stay over for a pajama party?"

"He could have given us a drink," Dru said. "I didn't like his attitude at all."

"When people are having a fight, they don't want company."

"He could have invited you in to wash up."

"Sure. Excuse me, Mrs. Dana; I'm sorry you're hysterical, but my hands are dirty and I've got to take a leak."

"I don't ever want to *see* him again!" said Dru. "You can go back and pick up the car by yourself."

"Thanks."

"Well, he was rude and you let him be."

"I let him be, folks. Did you hear that?"

"You did, Arch. When I told him we'd have to get our car off the hill before we could get the one he was loaning us down it, he said: 'That's *hardly* necessary. I *said* it was a Volkswagen.' You heard his tone of voice."

"Honey," Archie said, "the poor guy comes home from the office, see, an ordinary Wednesday night; he's had a hard day; he's not expecting company, much less his 'astro—'"

She interrupted him. "Don't make excuses for him . . . 'That's *hardly* necessary,' says he, 'I *said* it was a Volkswagen.'"

"Dru, he *knew* you were stalling around. You wanted to get inside that house, and he knew it!"

"Sure, I would have liked a drink, liked to sit down and calm my nerves."

"Liked to snoop," said Archie. "Sure."

"I have a right to be curious. I was invited out there!"

"*We* were invited out there, and we didn't have a right to snoop. You're a busybody; you always were. Remember how you used to go through my mail when we first met? That almost turned me off about you. It really did."

She said, "Do we have until tomorrow morning so I can go into the things that almost turned me off about you?"

"If tonight was anyone's fault," he said, "it was her fault."

"I was waiting for that."

"It *was*, Dru!"

"You'd defend Hitler, just because he was male."

"You haven't heard me defend him yet."

"The whole damn Nazi thing would turn out to be Eva Braun's fault."

"There *were* a few pretties like Ilsa Koch."

"See?" Druscilla Gamble said.

Archie dropped her in front of the apartment building and went to find a parking spot.

The doorman handed Dru a letter; Mrs. Muckermann had delivered it personally. It was addressed to Mr. and Mrs. A. Gamble, written in her almost microscopic script. Graphology was another of Mrs. Muckermann's enthusiasms. She had once loaned Dru a book on the subject and inside, heavily underlined, was a sentence which insisted that small handwriting was the sign of the deep thinker. Mrs. Muckermann had apparently put her name and address on the fly leaf before reading the book. Her handwriting there was large and florid, with circle i dots and exaggerated lower loops.

Dru made herself a Jack Daniels on the rocks, and changed into shorts and a shirt before reading Mrs. Muckermann's letter.

Dear Dru and Archie,

As I've warned Archie, the moon and Mars are in a square; he can expect arguments and disappointments, and I shy from adding to these bad aspects in his chart, but what must be done must be done regarding our project. I must now speak out, and I choose to do it on paper, hoping to keep the moon-Mars misfortune from flaring up, for violent scenes go with that trend.

On Monday when we lunched, Archie, at one point we were discussing the Mercury-Saturn opposition in your chart, which I politely, purposefully softened for you by saying it would cause distractions, since I see no point in alarming a person who has not come to me for advice. You looked at me, do you recall, and said, "I'm going to be distracted until 1974?" and your mouth bent in a snide smile? Was it merely a skeptical smile, or was it also a mocking one? It doesn't matter.

Druscilla, you will admit I have tried to protect Archie by not insisting he understand the truths revealed in his chart . . . and by not stressing the malefic indications there. I agreed with you: it didn't seem necessary.

However, Druscilla and Archie, it is obvious that much of the unconscious hostility brewing in Archie's sign is working its way out (inevitably, with these aspects!) and anyone who has any contact with you, Archie, will soon fall its victim.

Again, in the lobby of my hotel as we were engaged in conversation, it became clear to me, Archie, that you had not even bothered to read Astrology by Joseph F. Goodavage! And as I tried to help you compensate for this lack, by explaining to you about Hemmings and King George IV, your answer (so very "saturnine!") was, "Hum. Impressive."

I'm afraid I must say "Hum to you," as well, for if you do not find scientific knowledge worthy of your careful attention, you cannot impress my television viewers with anything you would write! I am not surprised. Your aspects are very self-destructive when they are not aimed against others!

Druscilla, I had hoped Jupiter would see us through, for he is so lucky when one knows how to use him. The point is Archie doesn't believe in using him, for Archie doesn't believe in him!

If it were not for you, Druscilla, I would be inclined to say there is no point in continuing; I would simply request another writer, for I have my own bad aspects to cope with, as well as Archie's (Mercury acting up again!), but I will proceed, if Archie takes these matters under advisement, and if—the big if—he can locate the astro-twins we so desperately need.

Sincerely as the<br>stars guide us,<br>Anna Muckermann

When Archie walked into the apartment, he was carrying a small blue and white Pan Am bag.

"Where did you get that?" Dru asked. She handed him the cold bourbon highball she had fixed for him as insulation against the Muckermann letter.

"What's this about?" he said. "I thought you were mad at me?"

"I'll tell you what it's about in a minute. Where did you get that?"

He slung the bag into the Boston rocker. "It was in the back of the car. I had to park 'way over on First Avenue. I locked up, but I was still afraid someone would slit the roof."

He took a sip of the drink. "I suppose I'm poisoned now."

"Right," she said. "What's in the bag?"

"I didn't look."

"Maybe he'll need whatever it is."

"I think it's her car, not his," Archie said. "I think the Falcon's his."

"The Falcon's hers," said Dru. "Brace yourself, Arch, there's a letter from Mrs. Muckermann on the coffee table."

"Oh? Why should I brace myself?"

"You'll see."

"And why is the Falcon hers?" he said, going across the room to get the letter.

"Because there's a penny on the door. I noticed it while you were talking to him, when we first got there. That's more like a woman, to stick a penny on the door." She walked over and picked up the canvas bag, unzipping it.

Archie said, "I gather you've read this, hmmm?" He sat down on the Queen Anne sofa with the letter in his hand.

"Yes, I did."

"*Nice*," he said sourly. " 'With what a dreadful curiosity, Does she launch out into the sea of vast eternity.' Christ, Dru, when are you going to knock it off!"

"The letter's addressed to both of us, Arch."

"I'm sorry."

"It doesn't matter." She felt a flip of surprise and vague excitement as she looked at what was beneath the female clothing in the flight bag. Letters bound with a rubber band, and a small black book with a gold inscription: D I A R Y.

Archie had come across and put his arms around her. "That was unfair of me. I'm sorry."

"Oh, go drink your poison," she smiled. "I'll put this in the hall closet."

"Anything in it?"

"Just clothes. It's hers, I guess."

"You're right, though," Archie said appeasingly, "it isn't like a man to put a penny on his car door."

She carried the bag as carefully as if she were sneaking off with found money.

In the bathroom she removed the letters and the diary and dropped them into the hamper. She was due for a long, hot bubble bath.

She heard Archie groan, "Oh my God! The moon and Mars are in a square; he can expect arguments and disappointment! Oh, *crap!*"

He was a slow reader.

She could not resist one quick peek at the diary, and she fished it out from the towels and Archie's shirts, opening it to a random page.

"*. . . but can I go on humiliating myself this way, without any semblance of character or integrity? Why can't I face what I've become? This isn't love! It's a cheap affair!*"

It seemed like Christmas, like getting three lemons in a row on a one-armed bandit, like shouting "Bingo!" or saying "I have a full house."

She threw the diary back into the hamper; it would keep.

But her face was as flushed as Archie's, whose cool was now on simmer as he turned to the last page of Mrs. Muckermann's letter.

**CHAPTER 8**

They planned that on Saturday Dru would follow Archie in a rented car while he drove the Volkswagen back to Grandview-on-Hudson. Their own car would not be ready for three more weeks.

When Archie phoned to tell Neal Dana that the Pan Am bag was safe in their apartment, Dana knew nothing about the bag; he thanked Archie anyway, saying it was undoubtedly his wife's. He added that she was visiting out of town and wouldn't be there for their arrival.

Thursday and Friday, like a fat woman sneaking secret snacks from the refrigerator, Dru Gamble fed on the diary and letters every time Archie was away from the apartment. He was still depressed about Mrs. Muckermann's letter and convinced he would not be able to come up with a usable pair of "astro-twins." He had given up on Neal Dana. He moped around the house more than usual, reading all the books Mrs. Muckermann had loaned him and listening to *Don Giovanni, Un Ballo in Maschera, La Boheme* and *Faust* on his tape recorder.

But when he would walk across to Pete's Restaurant for a

60

beer, or go out for cigarettes and magazines, Dru would run into the bathroom and retrieve the booty from the hamper, examining and re-examining it. Archie's rigidity on the subject of her "curiosity" and the individual's right to privacy stifled all her impulses to share the information with him.

The lover of Margaret Dana was unidentified except by a nickname. Most of his letters were written in pencil; his writing had a heavy pressure with very long t-bars and finals with hook ends. It was a large script which leaned to the right.

December. Wensday.

Dearest Virgo,

It's still a miricle about you're coming up to me that day saying would I help you that your car was stuck, and how all the fellas razzed me about the classy dame who drove me into work after my lunch hour was up, that day.

Marg, I'd like to dream the impossible dream as the song says because of you, and I know I'm no brain in your eyes like a psycollegist and what your used to, but Marg, I am a hard worker when I have a reason and strong. Marg, I am a good man and maybe I have made my mistakes in this life, but I have payed my debt to society and more than ever want to be straight for your sake, to show my appreciation for the trust you put in me.

Marg, I got an Xmas gift for you today and it is not much but Sweetheart I hope it will always remind you of yours truly— you will see why I say that soon (ha! ha!).

I miss you more than I did yesterday and less than I will tomorrow as they say but knowing your at my side is all I need to get thru life. I'll only sign this with all the love in my heart, Marg.

Her handwriting in the diary was small and vertical, but the t-bars flew high off the stems and the i's went undotted; it was an impulsive, emotional hand with long lower loops which touched the lines below.

15 December

Today Tuto (my all! He is my all!) presented me with the most delightful gift I have ever received. It is my Christmas gift, a funny, saucy, dear little black-feathered creature who is too human to be a parrot.

I have named him Sinister, since in astrology all left-handed aspects are so called, and Tuto is left-handed.

I am happy. I never wrote those three words nor spoke them with more conviction. I am happy! How incredibly easy-sounding that is, how simple it seems, and yet how alien this feeling was to me until that lazy Saturday afternoon in autumn when I strolled through Piermont and saw this Golden God with his golden hair and his strong shoulders, and that sure-footed gait.

Those dark eyes commanding my attention!

No, there is nothing easy or simple about finding happiness. It seems it was always there, but whenever I looked it in the eye, I would be frightened of its compelling brilliance, as ancient mortals feared to see the faces of their gods.

I do not mean to compare Tuto with "Diable" here. Three years ago I felt I wasn't good for anything because of my relationship with "Diable." But because of the love Tuto and I share, I feel unafraid and whole. "There is no fear in love; but perfect love casteth out fear."

"What's with you and these long baths?" Archie said on Thursday night.

"I've taken exactly three long baths. One last night, one this afternoon, and one just now."

"I know," he said. "What's it all about, Lady Macbeth?"

"'What, will these hands ne'er be clean?'" Dru said.

He put his arm around her and pulled her over to his side of the bed. "Look, honey, there's no point in two of us sweating over this thing. I placed fifteen more ads today, at my own expense; maybe we'll get a bite yet."

"Did you phone Mrs. Muckermann, Arch?"

"I wrote her. Don't worry. It was a very docile note."

"Of apology?"

He thought it over. "Yeah. There wasn't anything kiss-ass about it, though."

"Did you tell her you believe in Jupiter?"

"Yeah. Right." He laughed. "And Saturn and Mars and Mercury and Pluto. Oh, and Uranus."

"Don't be vulgar."

"I think it'll work out, honey."

She took his hand. "If there was only some way," she said, "of *making* Neal Dana cooperate."

January. Thursday.

Hi there Sweetheart,

Marg, this has been a busy day and I have not had all my shut-eye since last night I read a book called Hunza health secrets, about these people who live in the Hymalayas and live to be a hundred. Marg, you would enjoy this book for it is right up your ally. I am going to buy Yogert on my lunch hour for that is one of the secrets. They also exersise and practise Yoga. Marg, you should read this book and I will save it for you, since it is only a paperback and wasn't too expencive.

How are you, hon? I go to sleep dreaming of you and like my Italian name. I know a lot of Italians and they are all nice guys all though they like theyre wine. Marg, we will realise our dreams to run off to Rome and those places yet, for I am a pretty sharp poker player. You should ask the fellas I work with how much I rake in.

I have given it a lot of thought, Sweetheart, and I hate the idea he sleeps in the same bed with you. I know it is plain selfish since he is your husband and aparently such an o.k. guy, but what can you do about the green-eyed monster? I hope you don't like him as good as you like me that way, for I think that would kill me, and I would never be able to trust God or anyone again. I would be cureous to know some of the things he does to you that way, if you would ever care to tell me. (Only pulling your leg about that.) You are always in my thoughts, and I pretend my pillow is you and hold it as I dream sweet dreams. Your guy, Tuto, the wop. (Ha! ha!)

5 February

Miss Nickerson may suspect something. Today I was supervising the installation of the new storm windows when she came trudging up the hill in her arctics to ask me if I've noticed a prowler.

I said, "Oh, Minnie, it must be your imagination."

"Mother's seen him, too, on several occasions," she said.

"Well, I haven't seen any strangers," I answered.

"Then would you know who it is takes a walk up the side of the hill some afternoons, and cuts through the woods until he's out of sight?" she asked. "He goes toward your house, Margaret."

I said I knew of no such person; if there were such a person, I said, I would surely know.

She said, "That's why I came up to ask you about him. I figured you would know."

Yet the only safe way for him to come here is the back way!

I'll be glad when spring comes and the trees fill out and the foliage grows; it'll be easier.

I don't dare ask myself if there's any future in all of this. I feel so protective of Tuto, and so needed! I don't know what he'd do without me, and that's a beautiful feeling!

Friday morning Archie called CBS to find out about the possibility of getting an extension.

He hung up the phone and gave Dru a dark look. "No dice," he said.

"Why can't they shift their damn specials around?"

"Because," he said, "they're afraid this astrology craze is going to blow over."

"Oh, Arch, that's the most asinine thing I've ever heard! The newspapers have been carrying astrology columns for years and years!"

"And for years and years the newspapers have been dying out one by one," he said.

"Not because of the astrology columns! Are you on CBS's side or your own side?"

"I'm just telling you what they'd answer if I told them that," he said.

"People don't even have time to answer the ads you placed."

"I know," he groaned. "Some network vice-president sent around a memo pointing out how quickly the Maharishi Yoga fad went out the window, and they're all uptight now. *Jesus!*"

"Archie? Why don't you go for a walk, get some fresh air? You've been cooped up in this apartment too long!"

March. Sunday.

It's yours truly writing again, Sweetheart.

Well, Marg, I did a lot of research on Scorpio and learned all about myself last night and it seems I am in pretty good company, as they say, for some pretty sexy lovers have been Scorpios including Richard Burton, Rock Hudson, the late Senetor Robert Kennedy, and for women Princess Grace and Katharine Hepburn and that French singer Rita Piaff.

So watch out Marg, the women will be chasing me and what will you do if one of them ever catches me? Marg, I am only pulling your leg as I could never love another woman no matter how much she might have to ofer me. I am not a man who can be bought, even though the saying is every man has his price. Marg, this man doesn't and I want to tell you that right now, since you don't have that to worry about.

There is a girl who bowls out at the ally my team practises at, and she would like nothing better then to get my attention but I only laugh at her face, for in my heart I have my one and only.

Yesterday when I was leaving your place that nosy neighbur of yours watched me again. I thought you ought to know this information. Yours till hell freezes over, Tuto.

10 April

I can hardly blame Tuto, can I? He's a young man, and it isn't fair of me to expect him to sit home nights and pine over me. He didn't have to tell me, either. I would have had no way of knowing he was taking her to an occasional movie. Why shouldn't he? I would rather have him do that, than go drinking with the gang after bowling. If there were anything even slightly intimate about those "dates," I don't think he would have mentioned her to me.

Neal never goes out evenings. It's hard!

Friday night Liddy phoned, and Dru called in to Archie to pick it up in his study. Then she listened outside the door.

Archie said, "Oh, hi! I heard you were back in town."

Archie said, "Well, I'm pretty busy right now, Liddy. Can't it wait?"

Archie said, "I'm afraid it's going to have to."

Archie said, "I'm sorry but—"

Archie said, "I'm not hostile! I'm not in the least bit hostile!"

Archie said, "Goddamn it, Liddy, I have important work to do!"

"All *right*," Archie said, "I'll call you tomorrow."

He banged down the receiver.

Then he came into the living room and complained to Dru about it.

"You're not that busy, Arch."

"Well, what the hell's the big emergency?"

"How do I know, but why not go over there and find out?"

"And why can't she tell me over the phone!"

"Aw, it's just not the same," Dru said snidely.

"See what I mean? Damned if I do, damned if I don't."

"I don't damn you if you do. I have slain the green-eyed monster, darling."

"He was around the other night at '76 House."

She said, "I wouldn't care if you went over to see Liddy right now. I mean that, darling."

She did, too; by the next morning the diary and letters had to be inside the Pan Am bag.

Even when Archie didn't notice how long she spent in the bathroom, she felt too tense to read them comfortably when he was in the apartment.

"You know?" he said. "It might be a good idea to just get it over with. She claims it's wildly important."

April. Monday.

Hi Gorgeous!

Marg, I was dreaming today of us taking that camping trip we always talked about and wish it was possible. I would like to get away myself for it is sickening how some girls chase after a fella when he doesn't see them that way, which I certainly don't though she is a looker and a Virgo like you. My type, I guess, is Virgo.

There is no electricity there though, Sweetheart, so don't

worry your pretty little head over anything right now. She can try all her tricks but I'm not falling for any of them. Her uncle knows Frank Sinatra. Marg, what are we going to do about that dog, Marg? I couldn't get up there yesterday because of her as I said on the phone, and I really didn't honestly think you wanted me coming up the hill as you said over the phone, so I went on out to the ally to see what was doing their. Nothing much was but she showed up and rode me for about an hour about letting my hair grow. Marg, you never said do you like it? I'm going to have sideburns but not turn into Tiny Tim or anything. (Ha! Ha!)

Marg, my sister told me she sees Dr. Dana from time to time which is news to me, she just goes to Wethead Haven (as some call it) and pops in on him as she would say. She doesn't suspect anything about us, don't worry. He is a good guy and probably wants to help her, for she is a mixed-up kid with a bad temper that will get her in trouble yet.

Sweetheart those pincher dogs are mean and can kill people I hear. I don't like that dog. Hope we can find some way to get Dr. Dana to go out of the house to New York some nights like he thinks you do. For we have only one night a week which is not enough for a sexy Scorpio lover. Marg I'm eating lots of wheat germ for my verilitie so watch out! My new suit went over big at the ally thanks to you, and for everything. You have really changed my life you know that Marg. Love,

Tuto

1 May

I feel that the advertisement was a sign to me, showing me a way somehow. The stars will intercede; I can't explain why I feel that, but I do. Neal is so stubbornly against astrology; if CBS answers I will have to handle him with kid gloves. At least it will keep him occupied for awhile. I trust he'll have to to go into New York for it. I think I can persuade him to do it. There has always been a little of the ham in Neal. If his appointment at Doubleday goes well, I may convince him it would help sell books, become a "personality."

Dru was asleep when Archie came in; and Saturday morning, before she could ask him what Liddy had wanted, Neal Dana called.

"You're coming out today, aren't you?" he said. "This is Dr. Dana."

"We'll be there around noon, if that suits you."

"I think I've been pompous ass!" he said. "Why don't you and your husband postpone your visit until the cocktail hour? Around five-thirty?"

"We'd love to," Dru told him.

"Mrs. Dana is still away, but maybe we can all go out to dinner later anyway."

She said, "My husband's in the shower now, but I'm sure he'd like that very much. So would I," she added, feeling suddenly very sorry for Neal Dana.

Did he have any suspicions about his wife?

If he didn't, wasn't it wrong somehow to return the bag with the letters and diary inside, after Archie had told him of the bag's existence?

Because of Dru and Archie, he would have learned of his wife's infidelity; how would they set with him after that?

Neal Dana said, "I'll be looking for you, Mrs. Gamble."

"Call me Dru," she said.

She made a decision. The diary, the letters, were not going with them. She heard Archie singing "Addio alla madre" in the bathroom.

She went across the room to remove the evidence from the Pan Am bag, in which she had replaced it the night before. But the nightgown, the swim suit, the slippers? Leave them. The bag had to contain something.

Tuesday.

Greetings!

Marg, I know you're mad at me but I don't like that dog! She was there again yesterday when I tried to come to see you. I would have phoned but I knew you would be mad as a hornet so I'm writing this to leave in the mailbox pur usual. The news is I have to keep working an evening shift so even if you get more evenings I'll be working, except for the usual Wensday. Maybe I can change it if we could take a camping trip or get away. I wish I could take the black chariot in the garage and come and snatch you away suddenly, but would my name be mud. My nerves aren't so good. Marg, the truth is your boy is unhappy and I am mixed up about where we are heading and I don't think we'll ever get away to Italy or none of that. At the ally I get rode about not having a woman and even if I told them they would never believe me, but I would not do that so don't fret. They say why don't I take out some young girl and live it up like the lover I am, which is no refleckshun on you.

Well that is all for now except I love you but when are we going places and doing things never I bet. This girl from the ally says sock it to me, baby and fresh things like that which you would think vulger, but a lot of kids my age talk in such a way. Marg, I wish we could get away from all this. Love,

T.

7 May

I took a chance and called him at work last night, right from the same house with Neal upstairs, while my Italian record played. I wanted to say good-bye and couldn't; instead I promised him we'd go away within 30 days, somewhere if only for a brief few weeks. Somehow! Today he appeared with a gold pin for me, which he had saved to buy me. I could have forgiven him anything, it was so sweet of him. But in bed he began to tell me how that girl liked to be loved, claiming he had heard it from his gang at the alley. Oh, I know better, and I know how it excited him to watch the pained expression that must have been in my eyes. I love him, but can I go on humiliating myself this way, without any semblance of character or integrity? Why can't I face what I've become? This isn't love! It's a cheap affair!

Tonight the Gambles are coming from New York, and I'm "gambling" on them, and on the stars to intercede. I must have more time with Tuto if I am ever to sort out my feelings.

I know it sounds foolish, but I have the strangest feeling there is a way out through this "astro-twin" business. Something made me notice that ad! Fate!

"Are all the towels in the wash?"
Dru jumped at the sound of his voice.
Archie came dripping across the living room.
"What's that you're reading?" he wanted to know.

CHAPTER 9

Saturday afternoon Neal made himself a stiff gin and tonic before he telephoned Margaret's mother. Mrs. Kelly lived alone in a farmhouse outside Doylestown, Pennsylvania.

"Hi, Mrs. K.! How're you?"

"Neal? I'm all right. Where are you?"

"In Grandview."

"What's the matter?"

"Everything's fine . . . Is Margaret there?"

"Here? Why would Margaret be here?"

He said, "To tell the truth, Mrs. K., we had a small disagreement." He was reminded of his own observation about the phrase, "To tell the truth." People who used it habitually, habitually concealed the truth.

Mrs. Kelly said, "Margaret wouldn't pack up and leave over a small disagreement."

"She didn't pack," Neal said. "If she did, she didn't take much. I thought she might have run over to Bucks County for a few days."

"Did she take her car?"

"No, she couldn't; it wasn't here."

"Then how was she supposed to run over to see me?"

Neal said, "I thought she'd take the bus to New York, the train to Trenton, and have you meet her there, just as she did three years ago."

He took a swallow of his drink and watched a tanker glide through the blue waters of the Hudson. He felt a sudden wave of envy as he noticed the men on deck leaning lazily on the rail; he imagined the simplicity of such a transient existence and the easy camaraderie in a world away from women.

Mrs. Kelly said, "Are things as bad between you two as they were three years ago?"

"Not anything like that," Neal said. "We had a silly argument. CBS is doing a special about astrology. They were advertising for people born at a certain time, and my birthdate matched one they listed. Margaret sent in my name without telling me, and I lost my temper."

"I don't blame you, Neal," Mrs. Kelly said. "She's too involved in that nonsense."

Neal said, "This writer and his wife came here from New York Wednesday night. Margaret didn't tell me anything about it until the last minute. I refused to have anything to do with them. She was too embarrassed to face them, and she became hysterical, so I told them she wasn't home and got rid of them." He chuckled. "Or at least I thought I'd gotten rid of them. They had an accident on the hill. I had to lend them Margaret's car so they could get back to New York. She was damned angry over that."

"She had no right to be," said Mrs. Kelly. "It was her fault they came up that hill in the first place."

"She was furious just the same. She said, 'Now you've fixed it so I can't go anyplace. We'll see about that!'"

"What did she do?" Mrs. Kelly said.

"Nothing Wednesday night. She slept in the guest room, she was so teed off. I had an early appointment Thursday, and I didn't bother going in to wake her up. When I came home from work that night, she was gone."

"No note?"

"Nothing."

Mrs. Kelly said, "If you want my opinion, Neal, she's trying to worry you sick, to get even with you . . . She's not here."

He said, "Are you sure?"

"I promise. She's not here."

"I don't know where she could be, then."

"Neal?"

"What?"

"Do you have some gin and vermouth?"

"Sure."

"You go and crack some ice and make yourself a nice dry martini. Sit back and enjoy it. Have a second one when you're finished, and another one after that. She can just go to the dickens! Don't you worry about her."

Neal said, "But she's been gone for two and a half days!"

"Let her stay away a whole month! She'll come back. She did the last time, and she will this time."

"This isn't like the last time, Mrs. K.," said Neal. "Everything's fine between us."

"It could have been three years ago, too, if she hadn't been so stubborn. She's a very selfish girl, Neal!"

"I don't know," said Neal. "Maybe I was too bullheaded. It wouldn't have hurt me to talk with those people from New York. In fact, I invited them out for drinks tonight."

"You're playing right into her hands," said Madeline Kelly. "Oh, she always gets her own way; *always*."

Neal said, "If you hear from her, will you tell her that I've asked the Gambles for drinks?"

She sighed disapprovingly. "All right, dear. But she doesn't deserve you. If you want my opinion, Margaret's probably staying at some expensive hotel in New York, shopping and going to the theater, while you stew!"

"I hope it's something like that," he said.

"Oh, she's all right, Neal. She always lands on her feet."

After Neal hung up, he put on an old record of William Kapell playing Beethoven. Then he got Sinister's worms from the refrigerator and fed him supper.

"*Dov'è il consolato americano?*" Sinister said.

"Down the street," Neal said.

"*Dov'è una farmacia?*"

"Right next to the American Consulate," said Neal.

He looked forward to the Gambles' arrival. The day's depression was lifting, as it always seemed to toward evening when he made his first drink. Both Thursday and Friday night he had gotten quietly bombed up in his study, trying to work on his outline. Penny had kept their bargain and not telephoned him, though he suspected the half-dozen calls he had received since Thursday, when no one spoke, but the caller just listened to him repeat "Hello," had been from Penny. He had promised to call her in a week. He had explained that he wanted to plan his next steps very carefully and thoroughly . . . just when to start mentioning to colleagues that Margaret was gone, just when to notify the police. It would be a while before Penny and he could see each other; Neal didn't look forward to it.

The worst time of all was in the early morning when he woke up. Then all of it didn't seem possible, and he would find himself futilely picking away at the thing . . . why Penny had gone into the house when she had seen Margaret's car in the drive, why she had remained there after she saw Margaret, why she had had to needle Margaret about being barren, why, why, why . . . until inevitably it came down to why Neal had ever become involved with Penny Bissel.

He went into the kitchen to refreshen his gin and tonic and put the worms back in the refrigerator. Margaret was one of those women who never overstocked groceries. They had too much of everything else, from linens to liquor, but the kitchen shelves contained little more than staples like salt and sugar and spices, and in the freezer there were only rolls.

He would have to shop. There was so much he would have to attend to now: discover the day the dry cleaner called, the laundryman; garden and make the bed, clean, pay the bills. He couldn't advertise for a housekeeper yet.

While he worked the ice cubes out of the tray he listened to the crisp, descending fanfare of the opening theme in the Beethoven concerto. Margaret had taken Neal to hear Kapell the first year they were married, when they were living in New York. Kapell had played Schubert and Liszt, and Neal had been so impressed that he had gone to Goody's the next day to buy all his records. A few years later, Margaret and Neal heard over the radio one night that Kapell had been killed in an air crash. They had put on the record which was playing now: the *Concerto No. 2 in B-Flat*, and Rachmaninoff's *Rhapsody on a Theme of Paganini*. Tears had streamed down Margaret's cheeks as they listened.

He carried his drink into the living room and snapped off the hi-fi. There was no sense inviting melancholy. Every one of their records would remind him of some time with Margaret. He turned on the radio and found a rock station. Simon and Garfunkel were singing "Where have you gone, Joe Di-Maggio?" from their recording of "Mrs. Robinson."

Sometimes Margaret had called him "Joe" because of his resemblance to the baseball hero. He steeled himself against continuing in that vein. Life wasn't conspiring to remind him every second of Margaret; he was doing it to himself, playing in to it. He sat down, turned off the radio, and tried to think about his book, concentrating on the ideas he had gathered for the chapter on smoking mannerisms. But like a ghostly sound from some safe time when things were normal, he heard the honk of Margaret's horn as the Volkswagen made its way up the hill.

The Gambles were fifteen minutes early.

Archie Gamble sipped a Dewar's and water, sitting with his legs crossed and a hand on one knee. He was wearing black loafers and gray slacks, a light blue sports jacket the color of his eyes, a matching blue V-neck Shetland sweater under it, white shirt and black knitted tie.

"Astrologists," he said, "believe that everything is under the influence of the planets and signs of the Zodiac: animals, plants, precious stones, cities, even the Twelve Disciples of Christ."

"Tell Neal what sign Judas was," said Dru Gamble. She was dressed in a brown wool suit with a yellow scarf holding back her rust-colored hair; she was sipping a martini on the rocks.

"Judas was Pisces."

"No, Arch, he was Gemini. Your sign. Wasn't he?"

"I appreciate your confidence, Dru, but Judas was Pisces."

"Are you sure?"

Gamble shot her a dirty look. Neal interceded. "How did they come up with Judas' birthdate?"

"They didn't. You have to remember that both Judas and astrology were around before our calendar was devised." Gamble lit a cigarette. "The old astrologers believed that the Twelve Disciples were chosen to represent the twelve fundamental qualities. The ruling Trinity was the Sun (the Father), whose spiritual light (the Holy Spirit) was reflected by the Moon (the Son), flowing out through these dozen apostles into all of humanity, which was divided into the twelve basic types."

Neal said, "And which disciple *was* the Gemini?"

"James, 'the lesser.'" Gamble laughed. "Sorry about that . . . James was quite an eloquent preacher."

"A flapjaw," Dru said, "like all Geminis."

"What was Peter?" Neal asked.

"Aries, the fiery, impulsive rock upon which the Church was founded!" Gamble answered with mock authority.

She said, "Matthew was good old Capricorn. Tax collector. Politician."

Neal said, "Is that your sign?"

"Thanks a lot . . . When did you decide I was materialistic and power-crazy?"

"You wouldn't say that about Joan of Arc," said Archie Gamble, "and she was Capricorn."

"So's President Nixon," Dru Gamble answered, "and Barry Goldwater and J. Edgar Hoover; thanks anyway, but I'm a Cancer."

Neal said, "Which disciple was the Cancer?"

"Dear old home-loving Andrew," she said.

"And who was the Virgo?" said Neal. "Virgo's my wife's sign."

"Philip was."

"Lyndon Johnson's a Virgo, too," said Dru Gamble, "and so is Greta Garbo . . . hey, I'm getting good. I think I'll set up shop and give Mrs. Muckermann some competition."

"As if astrology didn't suffer from enough ill repute," Gamble said. "But let's hear more from my 'astro-twin.' What do we have in common, Neal?"

"I know one thing already," she said.

"What's that?" Neal asked.

"Neither of you mind freezing to death. I'm *cold*."

They took their drinks from the porch and moved inside.

By eight-thirty, Neal was getting crocked and hungry. He was planning to take them into Piermont for lobster at Sbordone's, or they were planning to take him: Gamble insisted that dinner would go on his expense account. But both Gamble and his wife were nursing along the last drinks Neal had made them; Neal had the feeling they wanted him to agree to be on the show before they left the house.

Gamble was balancing one of Neal's yellow legal pads on his knee, making notes with a Pentel, while his wife stood near Sinister's cage, trying to make the parrot talk.

"He sings more than he talks," Neal said, "but he's unusually quiet tonight."

Eventually he would give Sinister away, but not for a long, long time. It would be an admission that he never expected to see Margaret again.

Gamble said, "Well, so far, so bad. We ought to be able to find more in common than this." He read from a list he had made. "We're both only children. We've both been analyzed. We were both married for the first time in 1950. We're both insomniacs. We bought the same type of Constitution mirrors at auction. We both smoke Trues. We're both childless, and we've both lived in New York City most of our lives."

"And we were both Navy," said Neal.

"Yes, both Navy . . . Well, it's not very hair-raising, is it?"

Neal smiled. "Did you really think we'd have parallel lives?"

"Hell no!" said Archie. "But I said a few prayers that I'd be wrong."

"Keep talking," Dru Gamble said. "Maybe you'll come up with more." Then she gave Gamble a snide look and said, "Of course, there's a certain new piece of information which we might include. Archie just found out about it last night."

"What's that?" Neal picked up his own empty glass to fix himself a short one.

Gamble said, "Nothing. It's her liquor talking."

"Tell him what Liddy told you. Why not? Is it a secret?"

Gamble put on a thick Southern accent. "Liquor get loose from de jug, it talk mighty loud."

Neal stood holding his empty glass. "Maybe we'll do better if we get some dinner inside us."

"Yeah. Right," Gamble agreed, but he only took a tiny sip from his drink. He said, "Hey, I forgot to put down your writing."

"I can't pose as a writer, even if I do go along with this," Neal answered. Should he go along with it, on the assumption he'd seem to be doing anything to get Margaret back?

Gamble said, "If you're going to write a book, it's legitimate to point out the parallelism."

"I don't even have a contract yet."

"And before you sign one," Archie Gamble said, "you're going to get an agent. I want you to have a talk with my agent, Neal."

Neal walked toward the kitchen for a refill.

Dru Gamble was talking baby-talk to Sinister. "Want me to tell you a tecret, hmmm? I've got a tecret." It was the same way Margaret used to talk to him.

As the kitchen door was swinging shut behind him, Neal heard Gamble tell her to shut up.

Finally, around a quarter to ten, they were ready to leave. Neal and Archie were waiting outside on the porch while Dru used the bathroom.

"What I don't understand," Neal said, "is why you don't get a pair of real twins? I've read studies of twins who were separated in infancy: they lived in completely different environments, sometimes not even aware of each other's existence, but their lives turned out to be shockingly alike. Their personalities and habits were, too."

"It just isn't as dramatic," Archie said. "Every television viewer isn't a twin, but every television viewer has an 'astro-twin.' You see what I mean?"

"Yes. I get it."

"Besides," Gamble said, "real twins are often born ten, twenty or thirty minutes apart."

"Would that make such a difference?"

"Supposedly it'd make all the difference." Gamble took out a package of cigarettes. "If you'd been born at four in the morning, instead of three-thirty, you'd be a Gemini with Gemini rising."

"What am I now?"

"We're Geminis with Taurus rising." He passed Neal a True and lit it for him. "The sign that's rising at the time of birth is called the ascendant. Now, that great old wise woman, Mrs. Muckermann, tells me that the ascendant is as important as the sun sign. So Taurus is as important an influence in our chart as Gemini. You see?"

Neal shook his head. "I pass."

"I know," Archie Gamble laughed. "It's all very involved. That's why there are so many misconceptions and so little valid astrology."

"Is *astrology* valid?" Neal said. "You don't even believe that."

"I don't believe communism works either," said Gamble, "but I understand its theories. That's all that concerns me: knowing the subject."

"You have a reason. You have an assignment," Neal told him. "What reason do I have to get involved in all this?"

Gamble shook his head. "My first year out of college I was a salesman for a while. I was lousy at it." He took a deep drag on his cigarette.

"I can only think of one reason," said Neal.

"That's a start."

"It'd make Margaret very happy."

Gamble didn't say anything.

Neal said, "I suppose you know that she *was* here Wednesday night? You probably heard her crying."

"Yes." Gamble looked embarrassed.

"We had quite an argument about it."

"I'm sorry," Gamble said.

"She's away cooling her heels, and I'm beginning to weaken and think oh, what the hell, if it means *that* much to her." He looked across at Archie Gamble in the moonlight. "It's not going to kill me," he said.

**C H A P T E R  10**

A week later Mrs. Muckermann was due for dinner at six; at five Dru was in the kitchen lining up the ingredients for spaghetti carbonara when the doorbell rang. A glance through the peephole revealed Mrs. Muckermann's round blue right eye.

"It's me, sweetie, I'm early."

Under her breath Dru murmured, "Are you *ready* for this?"; she hadn't bathed or shaved her legs or had any rest since lunch. She took the chain off the door and opened it.

"I didn't think you'd mind," Mrs. Muckermann said. "You don't, do you, Druscilla?"

"I'm just surprised," Dru managed.

Mrs. Muckermann entered waving a bunch of rhododendron leaves. "These will look nice on your table," she said confidently, "and I bought some white wine I saw on sale at Penthouse Liquors." She thrust the packages at Dru. "Put the wine in the fridge, dear, so it'll be cold for dinner."

Dru felt perversely angry at the realization that white wine would go well with spaghetti carbonara; she went to do as Mrs. Muckermann directed, and Mrs. Muckermann tagged along behind her.

80

"Is Archie working?"

"Yes. He's in his study."

"Good. We can have a little talk by ourselves."

"I've got to take a bath at some point," Dru said, "but Archie will probably be finished soon."

"Let him work as long as he wants to, dear. We can go right on talking while you're in the tub. I'll give your back a scrub for you."

"Actually, I was going to shower," said Dru.

"Shower away then. The steam will be good for my complexion. It opens the pores."

Dru found a vase for the leaves, and Mrs. Muckermann took it out of her hands and arranged them on the coffee table.

"Do what you have to do," she told Dru. "Just step over me if I'm in your way."

"What I have to do is sit down and have a cigarette," Dru said. "I've been on my feet all day." She flopped full length on the couch while Mrs. Muckermann settled herself in the Boston rocker.

Mrs. Muckermann said, "Maybe your brassiere is too tight, Dru."

"Huh?"

"That could be making you tired. You know, the breasts correspond to Cancer, so you Cancers are particularly sensitive there. You should not bind your breasts too tightly." Mrs. Muckermann reached in her bag for a stick of Juicy Fruit. It was her habit when others smoked to chew gum.

Dru said, "I don't have a bra on."

"Then maybe you should put one on. Your breasts need more support than others; Cancers need a lot of support there."

"Mrs. Muckermann," said Dru. "I'm a thirty-two-A."

"Maybe you're just tired, dear," Mrs. Muckermann agreed.

For ten minutes Mrs. Muckermann complained that there were nothing but Italian restaurants in the Gramercy area—

six that she could count—and crankily Dru argued back that there was Yen King and Molly Malone's Pub, and the Hearthstone, and Joe King's Rathskeller. Mrs. Muckermann said she couldn't see herself enjoying dinner in Joe King's with all the beer-drinking college boys singing bawdy songs at the top of their lungs, and Dru thought to add that there was also the Old Forge steak house and the Gramercy Hotel.

"I'm not going to eat in my own hotel night after night," said Mrs. Muckermann.

"How about Max's Kansas City on Park," said Dru, amusing herself with the idea of Mrs. Muckermann sitting down to a steak amidst the yippies and the hippies and the jukebox roaring out rock.

Mrs. Muckermann said, "I don't know anything about it."

"Try it," said Dru.

"But what I really want to talk about," said Mrs. Muckermann, changing the subject, "while Archie isn't present to hear, is where Mars, Neptune and Leo are right now in Archie's chart."

"I suppose they're up to no good," said Dru.

"Dear, they're in the Fifth House," Mrs. Muckermann said.

"I've forgotten what that means." Dru had planned to fix a small antipasto to precede the spaghetti: salami, prosciutto, hot peppers and radishes served with grissini. She stretched her arms and decided to drop the antipasto from the menu.

"The Fifth House," said Mrs. Muckermann, "is the house of speculation, hopes, pleasures, schools, property values, and *offspring*."

"You mean we're going to get a rent increase? Lose hope? Our stocks are going down—not Occidental Petroleum again; what?"

Mrs. Muckermann said, "No, it's not bad. It's good!"

Dru debated whether it would be better for the world if Mrs. Muckermann had had children, in which case she'd stay off Dru's back about them, or whether it was better that Dru bear the cross and the world was spared little Muckermanns.

Mrs. Muckermann said in a conspiratorial tone, "*You* know what I'm talking about, don't you, dear?"

"We're going to win the lottery. Right?"

"Dru, do I have to spell it out for you? B.A.B.Y."

"N.O," Dru said, "T.H.A.N.K.S."

Mrs. Muckermann's eyebrows shot up. "You don't want a baby?"

Dru used her wits. "With that Mercury-Saturn opposition in his chart, and the moon and Mars in a square?"

"Is that what's stopping you?" Mrs. Muckermann clapped her hands together. "I thought you had misgivings for some reason. I've never met a Cancer yet who didn't long to be a mother . . . Dru dear, those aspects won't affect a baby; you must remember—"

While she was talking, Archie came out of his study behind her, saw her, made the motion of shooting himself through the head, and turned to go back inside.

Dru said, "Hi, darling! All finished work for the day?"

He hid the fist he was shaking at her as Mrs. Muckermann turned around to greet him. "Good evening, Archie."

"Don't let me interrupt anything," Archie said. "I was just going to get a beer and go right back to work."

"You do that," said Mrs. Muckermann.

Now it was Dru making signs behind her back: *Help! Please!*, with her hands fixed in a suppliant gesture of prayer.

"I'll see you later," Archie said, and Dru got up and blocked his entry to the kitchen.

She gave his cheek a hard pinch and said in a saccharine voice, "I want to get your beer *for* you, Arch. I'll bring it in to you."

When she did, Archie was sitting at his typewriter imitating Professor Higgins, singing: "I think you've got it! By God, you've got it!" He ripped a sheet of paper from the machine. "You want to hear it?"

"Archie, damnit, she's your guest! I want to take a bath."

"You should have thought of that when you first walked up and said hi-yah to that nace old lady in you'alls nace pravit pock over to Gram'cy Squa-yah."

"It's your show, Archie!"

"Is it my paycheck, or your paycheck?"

"Please!"

"That's good. Now try to put a little more sincerity into it." He came across and put his arms around her. "I'll entertain her, honey. But listen to this opener, hmm?"

"Okay."

"Somewhere out there, watching this program with you," Archie read, "is *your* 'astro-twin.' He was born the same year you were, on the same day, at the same time. Is your hobby painting? His probably is, too. Do you like modern furniture? He probably does, too. Have you got three children? I'll bet he has three, too. And right this minute if you're sitting there thinking 'Rubbish,' he's undoubtedly echoing that inner thought. The subject? Astrology. Part I. 'Astro-twins.' Yours . . . and as you'll see for yourself tonight, mine." Archie threw the paper back on his desk. "That's just a rough draft, but that's how I want to open. Like it?"

Dru said, "Except for one thing: Mrs. Muckermann won't like the 'rubbish' bit. It's too negative. Can't he be thinking something positive?"

He said, "You're right . . . Then I'll just lead into the fact I never knew Neal before I started researching the subject of 'astro-twins,' and how much alike we are and blah-blah, blah-blah."

She said, "And how you've both been married for nineteen years," sorry she had said it immediately after the words were out.

He threw up his hands. "Go win!" he said. "Goddamnit, I *knew* I shouldn't have told you one damn thing about what Liddy wanted the other night. Now, I *knew* that. All the way home I was fixing the old zipper good across my mouth because I *knew* somehow it'd all turn out to be my fault!"

What Liddy had wanted was to inform Archie that their divorce three years ago was illegal. Liddy had gotten it in Mexico, in her hurry to marry Moneybags, and Moneybags' lawyers had discovered it shortly after he had discovered someone to whom he would rather be married than dear lovely Liddy.

Dru said, "I take it back, Arch. I'm sorry."

"I know you're always sorry after, but you just can't stop! You can't drop it!"

"I'm not as nonchalant as Liddy, I guess."

Archie heaved a sigh. "She's not nonchalant about it *at all!* She's in a hurry to remarry, and she can't until we straighten this out!"

"Mrs. Muckermann's in there hell-bent on my having a bastard," Dru said. She laughed. "Oh, Arch, come on: I promise not to needle you any more . . . . I *like* living in sin! I feel like a hippie."

He gave her a thoughtful look. She was wearing her old shorts and one of the button-downs with the sleeves cut off at the elbows, and she was barefoot. He said, "You *look* like something from over Avenue A way. How are things in Tompkins Square Park? Get any good grass lately?"

"I'm *trying* to get to the tub."

"That'd be a start." He smiled. "Go on. I'll make out with Anna Awful while you're in the suds."

"Speaking of suds," she said, "that's the last beer. You'll have to call Arnold's if you want more."

Then she said, "Arch?"

"Hmmmm?"

"I've been thinking. I feel so sorry for Neal."

"So do I. And I also feel we'd better return those letters and the diary."

"He's so crazy about her, Arch. It'd kill him. Let him believe she's in a snit about the show. She wants him to believe that!"

Archie took a swallow of beer. "She's obviously gone off on a little trip with Golden Boy. I don't think she's coming back right away. I'd want to know if you were off camping with a lover."

"Oh how we camped," Dru sang, "on the night we were wed . . . No, dum-dum, we aren't returning the letters and the diary. What a short memory you have. You hated it when Bob Towers told you Liddy was playing around, and you hated Bob Towers for being the one to tell you. You haven't been friends with him since!"

"Somebody was bound to tell me eventually," Archie said.

"And Neal will find out eventually, too, probably. But if he learns about it through us," she said, "good-bye 'astro-twin.' He'd hate us, Arch!"

"Touché," he said. "With your brains and my looks, honey, we're going to the top of the ladder."

"So, I've been thinking," Dru said, "why don't we have Neal in on your birthday."

*"What?"*

"Well, it's his birthday, too," she said guiltily. She liked to go out on her birthday, or have a party—whoop it up. Archie liked her to cook a gourmet meal for his. He didn't like parties or other people around to share it. She said, "He'd have to spend it alone, Neal."

"Oh, hell, she'll probably be back by then!" He was irritated with her for suggesting it.

"You're right," she said. "Dumb idea."

"I feel sorry for him, too," said Archie, "but we can't adopt him."

"That's true," Dru answered. "We'll just use him and then drop him."

She hadn't planned on saying that; it had just popped out like the Liddy thing. Probably because of the Liddy thing.

Hostilityville.

Archie was frowning at her. "What did you just say?"

"Nothing."

"I heard you, Dru."

"I just feel so sorry for him."

Archie's tone was taut with repressed anger. "If Margaret isn't back by then, invite him."

She went over and put her arms around his waist; he was facing away from her, and he didn't change his position or acknowledge her embrace.

She said, "Arch? I don't want him. It was a dumb idea."

He sniffed the air. "You really do need a bath," he said snidely.

That mad, he wasn't going to make up for a while.

C H A P T E R  11

When Archie returned from walking Mrs. Muckermann back to the Gramercy, he buzzed the apartment from the lobby.

"Yes?" Dru answered.

"Mrs. Gamble?"

"Yes."

"Your husband's been taken to Bellevue; he went off his rocker suddenly."

She laughed. "Archie? Get us some ice cream."

He walked around the corner to Arnold's and bought a quart of strawberry and a quart of chocolate, Dru's favorite combination. He decided he'd have some, too; he decided no, he wouldn't; he was high, but he wanted to go on drinking.

When he arrived with the ice cream, Dru was in her nightie, stacking the dishes in the dishwasher. Archie put the package on the kitchen counter and imitated Mrs. Muckermann's twanging falsetto: "And, of course, Judy Garland, another famous Gemini, had that very same configuration when she lost her role in *Valley of the Dolls,* so you *see*, Archie, it affects the professional life."

Dru was laughing very hard. "Oh, but—what *was* it she said

about the way people look when Gemini is rising; what was *that?*"

"I know," he said, slipping back to the imitation. "A very famous physiognomist, John Varley, noted that even though Gemini is a beautiful human sign, many people born when it is rising resemble in their heads and necks various forms of goats, kids and deers."

"Oh, oh—yes!" Dru was holding her stomach.

"Gemini," Archie continued as Mrs. Muckermann, "is not only the patron of intellectuals, but also of egocentrics and lunatics, like George III."

Dru said, "Gemini is a violent sign."

"Gemini is a barren sign."

"Gemini," said Dru, "is a schizophrenic sign."

"Jesus!" Archie said. "She sure had it in for me tonight!"

"She's really a nasty old woman, Archie."

"Maud, she's really rotten to the *core*," said Archie, taking off on an old Noel Coward song, "it's funny that I never thought of it *before*."

"Do you want me to mix yours, or do you just want straw-berry?"

"I just want Scotch splashed over a few rocks."

"Oh, *Archie*."

"What?"

"You've had plenty. You've got to write tomorrow."

He said, "I'll finish the wine then."

"You already finished it. Mrs. Muckermann and I had a glass apiece; you had the rest."

"What did you serve wine with dinner for if you didn't want me to get smashed? I thought we were going to cut that out."

"She brought it. My God, Arch, didn't you hear her say she'd brought it? She must have said it a dozen times!"

"Fix me the Scotch, hmmm? I'm going to put on pajamas," he said.

As he went through the living room, the phone rang.

Neal Dana said, "Archie? I hope I didn't wake you people up?"

"We're night people. How are you, Neal?"

"Fine! I heard of a house."

"A house?"

"Dru said you were interested in renting a place out here for the summer."

"She did?"

"We were all pretty crocked. I don't blame you if you've forgotten."

That night had been the first time in years that Archie had been forced to drive with one eye closed so he could see the road.

He said, "Well, we've talked about it; what did you find?"

"A little place half a mile down, near Piermont. They're going to Europe; they'll rent it cheap if you look after their cat."

"What's it like?" Dru brought a Scotch in to him and sat beside him on the couch, close enough so they could share the receiver.

Neal said, "Rustic, two-story, two bedrooms and a bath upstairs, a big living room with a fireplace downstairs; kitchen, dining room. It's off the road, on a hill, surrounded by trees. Lots of privacy."

"How much?"

"Only two hundred dollars a month with the cat. The Cages are leaving a week or so before Memorial Day; they'll be gone until Labor Day."

Dru was counting on her fingers. She whispered. "Only eight hundred dollars, Arch!"

"How much is it without the cat?" They weren't his favorite animals.

"No deal without Tiffany. But she's a nice cat, Siamese."

"I love Siamese!" said Dru. She gave Archie one of her ardent, wistful looks.

"We'll have to talk it over," Archie told him. "How soon do we have to decide?"

"It's May seventeenth now. They'll have to know soon."

Archie said, "If it's such a good deal, how come somebody hasn't snapped it up?"

"They hadn't planned to rent it," Neal said. "The cat was going to her mother's, but her mother has very expensive furniture. She doesn't want the cat unless they declaw it. They refuse—soooo."

Dru was tugging at his shirt, mouthing the word: "Please?"

Archie said, "Can we sleep on it?"

"Sure . . . It's really a bargain for out here, Archie."

"I appreciate that. We'll call you tomorrow."

"One other thing," said Dana. "I have to come in for a part for my car: I need a new muffler. I'll probably run in next weekend. Do you want to get together?"

"Fine! Hey—I've got an idea," Archie said in a boozy burst of generosity. "It's our birthday a week from Tuesday. How about coming here to celebrate it on Saturday?"

Dru murmured under her breath, "*He's* got an idea, folks."

"I'd like that," said Neal Dana. "It's a date."

"If Margaret's back by then," Archie said, watching Dru make an obscene "up yours" gesture at the mention of Margaret Dana's name, "we'll expect her, too."

"I hope she'll be back," he said. "To tell you the truth, I'm a little worried."

Archie decided not to pursue the subject. He said, "I'd like to meet her," and then, "Okay, Neal. We'll talk tomorrow."

"Archie? Before you call tomorrow, can you do me a favor? I need the number of the English Ford dealer in Manhattan. I want to call him about the muffler, and information hasn't got a listing. Could you find out?"

"An *English* Ford?" Archie said.

"Yes. A Ford Consul."

Archie and Dru exchanged puzzled looks.

"I'll do that," said Archie.

"I appreciate it. Talk to you tomorrow," Neal Dana said.

Archie put down the receiver.

Dru said, "That was his car at the bottom of the hill that night."

"Who belonged to the Ford Falcon?"

"Where was the Consul last Saturday night?" Dru said.

"It could have been there. I didn't notice another car; was there one?"

"I don't remember," said Dru. "But he drove the Volkswagen to dinner. We followed the Volkswagen."

"Ummm. If he had a bad muffler, it might have been in a garage."

"But who owns the Falcon? . . . Arch, Tuto mentioned a 'black chariot.' The Falcon was black," Dru said. "Could Tuto have arrived on the scene suddenly? Could that have been the reason everything was so peculiar?"

"Try this," Archie said. "Something came up that caused Margaret Dana to want Neal out of the house. She sent him for champagne. But Dana suspected it was a ruse. He left his car at the bottom of the hill and waited. Tuto arrived and he caught them red-handed."

"Caught them doing what? They wouldn't do anything with him due back."

"Maybe he caught them as they were getting ready to take off. In the middle of the scene, we arrive."

"But Margaret Dana *knew* we were on our way."

"Didn't Tuto say he felt like just coming up to snatch her away? Maybe he made good his promise. Or maybe Margaret Dana *picked* that moment to take off. Neal would come home and find us there. In the confusion, Margaret and Tuto would have a head start," said Archie. "But Neal fouled up the plan by sneaking back and catching them."

"Then Tuto would have been there when we arrived."

"They could have all been in the midst of a real ruckus!"

"And then?"

"Then when Neal got rid of us, Margaret and Tuto took off."

"And Neal knows all about it?" Dru took a gulp of his Scotch.

"It's possible. There *are* loose ends, though. Why was her bag in the Volkswagen?"

Dru said, "If a woman's running off with a man, she doesn't take just a nightgown, slippers, and a swim suit. That's packing for a motel, Arch. Motels all have swimming pools now. I think she just kept that bag in her car, kept the letters and the diary in it, and only used it when they rendezvoused away from the house."

"Did they rendezvous away from the house?"

"How would I know?"

"How would *you* know! You all but memorized the letters and the diary—you read every word half a dozen times!"

"You read them, too," she said.

"Not the way you did, love," he said. "Hey, that's *my* drink. Leave some for me, Laura Lush."

"Something was terribly wrong that night. But I don't know if it had to do with Tuto."

"We could be 'way off base. The Falcon could belong to a friend."

"A Falcon," Dru mused, "with a penny on the door."

"That's right; I remember your mentioning that."

"It isn't much like a man to put a penny on his car door, but a boy would do it."

"How do we know Tuto's a boy?"

"Come on, Arch: he was all concerned about growing his hair long; he wrote about 'kids' his age."

"Yeah." Archie took his drink away from her and frowned as he thought about it. "I *don't* think the fight could have been about the show. Neal doesn't impress me as someone who'd raise hell over something so silly."

"And he's consented to do the show."

"Well, he claims his reason for that is to please her."

"I just don't get it."

"'The stars will intercede,' she wrote, and they seem to have obliged her, one way or the other."

"Oh, and *I* did the memorizing."

Archie said, "He must be cooperating with me to please her. It's the only reason I can think of for his going along with it."

"And if he wants to please her, he couldn't know about Tuto."

Archie said, "That's not necessarily true."

"Then he's the masochist's masochist."

"Or he's in love with her. He sounds as though he is."

"If he knows about Tuto and he's still in love with her, and still wants her back, he's the masochist's masochist."

"In nineteen years, you can get attached," said Archie.

"To that extent?"

"Sure, to that extent. Don't judge everyone by what you'd do."

"Methinks you're just a trifle defensive suddenly."

"So I'm defensive."

"I'd forgotten about all the horseshit you took from dear old Liddy."

"Dru, don't start."

She imitated him. "In nineteen years you can get attached."

"Leave Liddy out of it."

"I'm all for leaving Liddy out of everything!"

But she was already started.

She said, "Why didn't she tell you what she had to tell you over the phone? Oh, no! She had to make a big deal out of it!"

"She didn't want to upset you, as a matter of fact. She wasn't sure I'd want you to know about it until it was all straightened around."

"Why? Doesn't she think we're close?" Dru got up and marched across the room for a cigarette.

"She thought you might have a bad reaction to it, though

*how* she could have come to *that* decision, I'll never know," he said sarcastically.

"Bull, Archie! She wanted to get you over to her place."

Archie said dryly, "I'm so thankful you think I'm such an irresistible, compelling—"

Dru broke in, "And you went running the very night she called!"

"Dru, you told me to go; you wanted me to go!"

"I was testing you, Gutless! I thought you might be able to resist Miss Big Boobs, but oh no! You flew out of here!"

Archie got up to go across to her and stumbled on the leg of the coffee table.

"And now you're drunk!" she shouted. "Look at you!"

He said, "I'm loaded because I didn't get anything to eat! Spaghetti, salad, pears and cheese; do you call that dinner? What happened to the antipasto you were going to make?"

"Mrs. Muckermann happened to it! Okay?"

"It was your idea to have her for dinner!"

"I did it for you, Archie, and you know damn well I did it for you!" There were tears of rage in her eyes as she stormed toward the bedroom, tossing over her shoulder the one-word anathema: *"Gemini!"*

Later, when Archie went into the bedroom, she was in bed, turned toward the wall. Archie got out of his clothes, didn't bother putting on his pajama pants, and crawled in beside her.

"Honey?" He put his arm around her waist.

She didn't answer.

"Maybe it would be good to get away from New York," he said, attempting to bribe her into responding.

His second attempt at bribery didn't work, either; she took his hand off her thigh and gave him a swift kick in the shins.

Archie fell asleep convincing himself that he would remember to write down tomorrow this new flimsy parallelism: both Neal Dana and he had owned Ford Consuls . . . Still, the English Ford wasn't all *that* common; it wasn't as if they'd both owned some American make.

He had a tossing, twisting night of darkness filled with the sight of Dru's face contorted in anger, long hallways with Liddy waiting at the end of all of them, and the sound of his own voice raised with rage, until a policeman named Saturn arrested him for the murder of Anna Muckermann.

Dru's voice asked plaintively, "Why did you do it, Neal?"

CHAPTER 12

The Friday before his birthday, Neal Dana left his house at eight-thirty in the morning and came face to face with Miss Nickerson at the top of the hill.

She had Kendal, the Doberman, on a lead, and neither of them looked very happy to be there. They were positioned by the Volkswagen. Kendal growled, but Miss Nickerson had the good manners to force a "Good morning," and then she came right to the point.

"Where's *Mrs.* Dana these days, Mr. Dana?" she said.

Her bluntness threw Neal off guard; he had never thought of her as a nosy neighbor.

He said, "She's away, Miss Nickerson. How have you been?"

"Uncomfortable."

"Oh? Maybe Kendal's too much for you to handle. It must be quite a strain holding her back that way," said Neal, tossing his briefcase into the front seat of the Volkswagen. Kendal eyed him with hatred.

Miss Nickerson said, "I bought Kendal so I could be comfortable, bought her when I first saw that prowler."

"What prowler?"

97

"Mrs. Dana didn't tell you?"

"No."

"There's been some character hanging around these woods since the beginning of winter."

"Somebody hunting rabbits, maybe?"

"He's not a hunter. Mother and I think he's a Peeping Tom," said Miss Nickerson. "It got so we wouldn't sit in the downstairs unless the shades were pulled. Even in the daytime. Your wife didn't tell you this?"

Neal supposed it had probably amused Margaret as much as it did him: the idea of some poor fellow freezing his balls off in the winter, and risking encounters with rattlers and copperheads in the spring, for a glimpse of Minnie Nickerson and her mother tatting in their front parlor.

"She didn't mention it," said Neal.

"For a while I thought Kendal had scared him away, but he's been back twice in the past few weeks."

"Well—" Neal began.

"Oh, I'm not imagining it, if that's what your grin's about. Kendal chased him up a tree one night."

"*Really?*" Neal said.

"And the Saturday night following that, he was right on your front porch."

"Miss Nickerson," said Neal, "I had company that night. I didn't know you'd come up for a visit," he said diplomatically, angrily wondering how often she "visited," "or I would have invited you in. That was a friend of mine on my porch."

"Oh, no," she shook her head. "I wasn't snooping, either. I was walking Kendal and I saw him head up the hill on foot. Your company arrived in a car. I always know when you have company, because they always give a little honk before they go up the hill. But this was quite a time after the honk. Your company was already there. I saw your wife's car go up, the Volkswagen here, and the one following it with the redhead driving. She had on a yellow scarf."

Archie in the Volkswagen; Dru driving the rented car. Neal lit a True. He said, "Go on."

"I saw the prowler walk up the hill," she said, "and I decided to do a little investigating. I took Kendal and we followed him. We didn't get too close to him, but I saw him looking in your windows. He was standing on your porch."

Neal said, "Why didn't you call the police, Miss Nickerson?"

"Because of what they think of Mother and me. They think we're a pair of old women who imagine things."

"Then you should have called me," Neal said. He decided that either the police were right in their estimate of the Nickersons or some neighborhood kid had been poking around. One night last summer Neal had caught three of them skinny-dipping in the pool near midnight.

"I wanted to call you," said she, "but Mother said he might come down to our place then."

"Thank you for telling me about it," said Neal. "Can I give you and Kendal a lift down the hill?"

"No thanks. Kendal needs exercise. We'll walk down."

Neal got in behind the wheel. He said, "If you see him again, call me. I'll see that he doesn't bother you."

"There's been a car driving slow by your turn-off down on the road, too."

"Next time when you see something like that, just call me," Neal said. He put the key in the ignition.

"This car's black. It drives real slow, like someone was looking up at your place." Then she added, "I don't know what there is funny about it."

"I was just smiling at Kendal," said Neal. "She's a good dog, isn't she?"

Neal chuckled as he rode along River Road, deciding to tell the Gambles about Minnie and her mother and Kendal tomorrow night when he had dinner with them. Archie and

Dru had made a quick decision and moved into the Cages' house yesterday. Just before Neal arrived in Piermont, he gave a glance up at the house. No signs of life. They were probably sleeping late. Neal had dropped in on them last night after work and found them fairly well settled, except for the unpacking of Archie's dozen crates of books. They had invited him to have a drink, but though he felt the same early evening loneliness which was plaguing him since Margaret's death, he refused. He was not going to take advantage of their propinquity and lead them to believe that now they were near, he would always be underfoot.

He had had a taste of loneliness three years before when Margaret had been in Bucks County. That was bad enough, but he had tolerated it by believing that she would return. It was that same temporary loneliness which overtakes a man when his wife and children are at the beach in the summer and he's in the city. He had heard his colleague, Cliff Bates, complain about it often enough. Cliff's wife took winter vacations as well. There was a period some years back when Cliff had all but lived with Neal and Margaret. Neal had complained bitterly after a while; Cliff had even taken to staying overnight. Neal would wake up first thing in the morning and hear Cliff and Margaret disporting themselves out in the pool. Then Cliff would sit across from him at breakfast, return in the evening for cocktails and dinner, drinking sufficiently after dinner for Margaret to suggest it was unsafe for him to drive.

Neal had not been able to understand it. Was the man a complete jellyfish without his wife and daughter? Were they all there was to his life away from Rock-Or? Didn't he have other interests, or other friends besides Neal and Margaret?

Now he understood all too clearly. Nineteen years of marriage was an island. You visited and were visited by the mainland as a couple. The three friends who had called since Margaret's death had all expressed their desire to "get together when Margaret returns."

He had imagined that he would mourn more for Margaret, but again, because this time he knew she was not returning, her absence affected him much differently. He did not miss her. It was himself he missed, and having some sort of identity after five o'clock. He drank alone, ate alone, listened to music alone, and began slowly developing the unresilient, knotty little habits of a person living alone. He cleaned the house too often, began checking the evening's television fare in the morning when he read the *Times* (finding pathetic gratification when a good movie would be listed), and he jammed the freezer with Swanson's four-course frozen dinners and the cupboard with S.S. Pierce canned roast beef and chili, soups and puddings. He worked in the yard every night until it was dark; he installed "quiet" switches on all the light fixtures, as Margaret had begged him to do for years; he scraped and repainted furniture, fixed leaks, repaired screens, removed old window caulking and rearranged his library alphabetically.

He put off nothing that he could accomplish physically, but he became a mental procrastinator. He put off explaining to anyone any more than the fact that Margaret was "away"; he put off going to the police to report her absence. He put off planning or plotting his way out of it, and he put off Penny. Even his unconscious mind cooperated with him, for he had no dreams of Margaret that he could remember, nor any of Penny. The only woman to appear in a dream since Margaret's death had been Druscilla Gamble. She had run toward him in slow motion through the elephant grass, called him "Joe," as Margaret used to, and presented him with an apple.

At the clinic there was a letter from Doubleday waiting on Neal's desk. The editor was impressed with the outline; he wondered if Neal was free for lunch one day next week.

In the midst of Neal's elation, the telephone rang. Penny.

"I have a wonderful idea, Neal. I'll fix you a birthday lunch today."

"I can't come there."

"No one has to know. Leave your car in the Grand Union lot. Go in the back entrance of Woolworth's and use the underground passage to our building. You just have to walk up one flight."

"What about your father?"

"He's not here, Neal. He took the bus to Spring Valley to see my aunt."

"Penny, it's too big a chance to take." Last week, Cliff Bates had laughed when Neal had remarked that the switchboard girl listened in on his conversations. Neal had been testing to see if it were possible, and Cliff had relieved his mind by saying there wasn't a chance. "But aren't you getting a little paranoid, old man?" he had added.

Still, Neal didn't like these phone conversations.

Penny said, "Daddy's going to be gone until after dinner. He's going to call me before he leaves Spring Valley so I can meet his bus. It's safe, Neal. I won't get another chance to have you here for months!"

"I just can't see it. It's too risky."

"Neal, I have to see you. I haven't seen you since—" She couldn't finish the sentence.

"I know. Be patient. Pen, I'm doing everything I can to speed things up. But we need time."

"What are you doing?"

"What?"

"What are you doing to speed things up?"

"I can't go into it on the phone."

"It's too big a strain on me, Neal! I have to see you, Neal! I'll crack! I have things to tell you! I have to see you!"

"Listen, Pen—"

"You listen for a change. Do you know I drive by your house nights? I do, Neal! Hoping to get a glimpse of you, or hoping maybe you'll drive down the hill, or walk down to get your newspaper out of the mailbox."

"How can you get a glimpse of me from down on the road?"

"I could. Maybe see you up in your yard."

"Penny? You've never walked up the hill, have you?"

"No. I've wanted to, though."

"And you don't call and listen to me say 'Hello?' without saying anything?"

"No. I told you I wasn't doing that."

Neal didn't believe her; if Penny wasn't making the calls, who was? And if Penny had been wearing slacks that Saturday night, would Minnie Nickerson know from a distance whether it was a man or a woman?

Now Neal was concerned. What if she were like her brother, who made such obvious errors when he committed his petty thefts, that even the police observed he was more interested in the punishment than the crime? Penny repeated, "I'll crack, Neal."

"What time shall I come?" he said.

"You're *coming?*"

"Yes. About one?"

"Any time. Any time, Neal! Come before one if you want."

"I can't come before one."

"Oh, Neal! I feel like the world's off my shoulders."

"Just calm down. Everything's going to be okay, Pen."

"Neal? What do you want to eat?"

"It doesn't matter."

"It does! It's the first meal I've ever fixed you! I don't know what you want."

"A sandwich."

"No, Neal! I want to fix you something good. It's your birthday next Tuesday!"

"I don't care, Pen."

"Meat? What kind of meat?"

"Hamburger. Something simple."

"Neal, I'm so relieved! It's been a terrible strain. I have something to tell you. Oh, Neal, I'm dying to talk to you! Can you stay for a while? I mean, you won't run in and out in an hour, will you? Can you stay long?"

"Not too long," said Neal, who knew that as soon as he was there it would seem too long.

Neal's secretary brought him the BISSEL, FORREST file.

Neal needed to refresh his memory on certain points. When he came to the relevancies, he ran his finger under the words slowly, as though he were underlining them in his thoughts.

> Both parents were needlessly punitive and seldom touched or handled the boy except to punish him. His delinquent behavior was a way for him to attract their attention. As an adult he repeated this pattern, seeking the reprimand of authority by his larcenies. He invited punishment.

> The puritanical attitude his parents had toward sex compelled him to rebel and repent simultaneously. He was promiscuous from an early age. Guilt forced him to end his relationships soon after they had begun, and near the end of each one he would invariably go on a shoplifting spree, hoping to be caught and punished for the larger crime of having indulged in sexual intercourse.

> An interview with his only sister revealed that she also suffered the same treatment from the parents. More stable than he, with no record of delinquency nor any conscious antisocial impulses, she did confess she had an uncontrollable temper, and sometimes burst into violent rages during which she feared she might hurt someone "without even knowing it."

"Busy, Neal?" Cliff Bates' voice.

Neal looked up, closed the manila folder and waved Cliff to the armchair near Neal's desk. "No. Have a seat."

Cliff was one of these boyish fellows in his late forties who looked and behaved as though he were an aging relic of the Now generation. He tooled around in a red Mustang, bought his clothes at the University Shop at Saks Fifth Avenue, accompanied himself on the guitar while he sang Dylan and Donovan, and seasoned his conversation with generous references to his own amazing sexual prowess. Back in the time when he was so often at the Danas', Margaret had nicknamed him "Diable," and Neal would hear them giggling over their Scrabble games nights when he retired ahead of them, and hear Margaret call out, *"Diable à quatre!"* as she lost a game to him and had to pay the dollar.

"Carla and I haven't seen you and Margaret in a dog's age," he said, lighting his pipe. "How about coming by for Sunday brunch?"

Neal regarded him thoughtfully; he was going to have to start somewhere, with someone, and Cliff had known all about the thing three years ago. Margaret had left, in fact, shortly after Cliff had begun cutting down his visits to them. Cliff had kept her preoccupied; without him to take morning swims with her, without the nightly jokes and games and guitar sessions, she had begun to flounder. Neal's pleasure in Cliff's absence had soon faded and he had found himself actually asking Cliff when he was dropping in again, but Carla had returned by then from her European tour; Carla wasn't that mad about the Danas.

Neal said, "Cliff, I'm afraid Margaret's left me again."

Cliff removed the pipe from his mouth and grimaced. *"What?"*

"It looks that way," said Neal.

Then Neal gave Cliff the same version of Margaret's disappearance that he had given Margaret's mother. Cliff listened, too embarrassed to meet Neal's eyes, and when Neal was finished, Cliff's first reaction was a heavy sigh.

Neal said, "I think I'm going to the police about it, Cliff. She's been gone over two weeks now."

Cliff Bates' adamantine response surprised Neal. *"Absolutely not*, Neal," he said. "I agree with her mother. Margaret always lands on her feet. She's just giving you the business."

"It isn't like her, though, not to let me know where she is," said Neal.

"Isn't it?" Cliff said.

"No. It isn't."

Cliff got to his feet. "She'll be back," he said. "You'll see, she'll turn up." He gave Neal a reassuring punch in the arm. "And when she does," he added, "you have a date with the Bateses."

CHAPTER 13

You pushed Margaret, didn't you?, he thought.

"Neal?"

"What, Pen?"

Margaret didn't step back accidentally; she knew her own house too well for that.

"You're so quiet. What are you thinking?"

Was it true that Penny had wanted the showdown with Margaret? She had seen Margaret's car in the yard; why had she gone on in, and then *remained* after she saw Margaret? . . . remained to provoke her. What other reason would there be for her to stay there?

"I was wondering," he said, "where you ever found the recipe for this?" It must have been concocted by the makers of Gelusil, Bromo-Seltzer, Amitone, and Brioschi; chicken, underdone, swimming in a sour-cream, chicken-broth sauce, liberally treated with curry powder.

At one-fifteen in the afternoon!

She said, "I clipped it out of a magazine."

Served over noodles with creamed onions, white bread already buttered, and chunks of iceburg lettuce bathed in a bottled French dressing.

"You're awfully quiet, Neal."

"I'm eating, Penny."

"You're not eating very much."

"I don't eat a lot at noon."

"You ate a whole steak that day we went to '76 House."

"I hadn't had breakfast that day."

"Have some bread, Neal."

"No thanks."

"I buttered it for you."

"I really don't want any."

"Would you rather have rye bread, Neal? I've got rye bread, too."

"No bread, thanks."

"I should have bought rolls instead."

"Everything's fine."

"You ate a lot of rolls that day at '76."

"I hadn't had breakfast that day."

"Did you have breakfast today?"

"Yes."

"What'd you have?"

"Hmmm?"

"What'd you have for breakfast?"

"Bacon and eggs."

"Did you fix them yourself?"

"I stopped at the diner."

She wore light pink fingernail polish; it was chipped, her nails were chewed.

Margaret's hands had always been so impeccably manicured, graceful hands with long fingers which performed gracefully. Would she have used those hands to slap such an inconsequential face as the one Neal saw across the table from him?

Penny's lipstick was too dark; she wore mascara on both her upper and lower eyelashes. It was black mascara, applied so thickly that the lashes were glued together. She wore eye-liner; she had made wings at the corner of her eyes.

Had her makeup always been so garish?

In his memory she had seemed so young and wholesome and vulnerable that day on Bear Mountain when she had run toward him in the field of elephant grass.

"Save room for dessert, Neal."

"I won't be able to eat dessert, Penny."

"You have to, Neal. I bought it for you."

"I'll try."

"Neal?"

"What?"

"We're strange together. Can you feel it?"

"Feel what?"

"Like the way we act together. Like strangers."

"It's natural, under the circumstances."

"Is it?"

"Yes."

"Like you're the psychologist, you ought to know."

"In time everything will be all right."

"Will it?"

"Sure."

"The way it used to be with us?"

"Why not?"

The tablecloth was oilcloth; the napkins were paper.

Remember the way Margaret had set a table? There was always clean linen and often fresh flowers. Margaret would never place a milk container on the table, as Penny had done, or a tin of Durkee's black pepper alongside the salt shaker.

Neal had married Margaret when she was Penny's age, but even in the beginning Margaret had known the way to do things. She had been raised in an environment no more privileged financially than Penny's, but she had come from solid old Pennsylvania Dutch stock on her mother's side and God-fearing Irish Catholic on her father's. Blood will tell. Margaret had learned a sense of responsibility—yes, and the words she had cried out before she had plummeted to her death: *character, integrity*—she had had both.

But Bissel blood?

Neal remembered the wry grin that always tipped Forrest Bissel's lips whenever Neal reviewed with him his felonies and misdemeanors, the casual admission, "I'm not much good, am I?," and the shrug of his broad shoulders, as though there were nothing he could think to do about it, no way for him to fight it, nor a reason to.

And *was* there a reason to, when he received so much gratification in the punishment?

Now, supposedly, Forrest understood that there were other, better forms of gratification; supposedly Neal had given him the necessary insight to fight his behavior pattern and helped him gain the impetus for the battle. Time would tell how successful Neal had been.

Forrest had said, "From here on out, I'll think of *you* as my old man, my authority figure; that'll keep me straight."

Penny said, "I hate it this way, Neal!"

"I know."

"No, you *don't* know! I imagine that this," she hesitated, "this *thing* has turned you against me! Is it my imagination?"

"Of course it is."

"Is it?"

"I said *yes; it is!*"

"Don't shout at me, Neal. I can't take much more!"

"What's this all about suddenly, Penny?" He put down his fork and stared at her. Her face was red; she was close to tears.

"You don't even call me endearing names any more!"

"Oh, honey—"

"That's the first time!"

"Honey, listen, listen." He scooted his chair over next to her. "We both feel the strain. Pen, we knew it wouldn't be easy;

we knew we'd have to go for long stretches without seeing each other, we—"

"Stretches? You mean we'll only see each other off and on?"

"We can't just start seeing all we want of each other, Penny." He put his arm around her shoulders and the gesture made her burst into tears. He sat there stroking her hair, wondering what would have happened if he had called the police that Wednesday night. Could there have been a way for them to know he had not been any part of it, some advanced police technique that would have told them as much? Then it would be for her to prove her innocence, to convince them she had not laid a hand on Margaret. There would have been a scandal, yes, inevitably, but wouldn't it have been better to have gotten it all over with?

He would have lost his job at Rock-Or, no doubt; Doubleday would probably have disassociated themselves from him; but there would be no necessity to continue living this lie with Penny, no necessity to have to touch her. Good God, he could never touch her that way again, could he? Never. He could barely caress her now, when his life depended on it. He was stricken with disgust at the shoddiness of the scene, and the feeling of her warm tears running down his fingers as he lifted her face to his was as repugnant to him as if they were urine.

"Honey, look at me."

"What?" she said weakly.

"I want you to be strong for me. I want you to promise me you'll get hold of yourself for me. You're important to me, honey. Don't you know how important you are to me," he intoned, "how much it means to me that you're safe and happy? What's this whole thing about, if it isn't about that, hmmm? Don't you understand how I feel about you?"

"Do you love me, Neal?"

"Oh, Pen, don't you know?"

"Yes, but, I like it if you say it," she said sniffling. She wiped away her tears with her knuckle, and the black mascara was smudged down her cheek.

"I love you," he said.

"I bought you a birthday cake and you said you didn't want any dessert," she whined. "Didn't you think I'd buy you a birthday cake?"

"I didn't think, honey. Thank you for going to the trouble."

"You see what I mean?" she whimpered. "We're so darn formal with each other, like don't thank me for going to the trouble. A lover *does* that for her lover's birthday, Neal."

"You're just very sensitive, Pen. Maybe I'm not sensitive enough, but I appreciate it, honey. I really do."

She took the paper napkin from her lap and blew her nose with it.

"And I bought you a record," she said. "Classical. Because I know you like that type music."

He forced himself to press his lips against her forehead.

She said, "I bought you *Claire de Lune*. Do you have it?"

"No, I don't. Oh, honey, that was very sweet of you. You shouldn't have done that."

She began to cry all over again.

"Why are you crying, Pen?"

"A lover *buys* her lover a birthday gift, Neal, don't you *know* that?"

"I'm glad you did it, Penny. I've always liked *Claire de Lune*."

"There are other things on the record, too," she managed, trying to get control of herself. "It's a long-playing classical." She blew her nose again, and her moist left hand clutched at Neal's. "You do love me, don't you?"

"Yes."

"Really?"

"Really."

"Because I have to tell you something."

"What?"

"I don't know what you're going to say, so I'm afraid."

"Try me," he said. "Oh, honey, you don't have to be afraid of telling me *anything*. We don't have secrets, Pen. My God, we *can't* have secrets from each other." He gave her shoulder a gentle squeeze. "Just tell me, Pen; don't worry about it."

"Neal?"

"What?"

"Neal, I'm two weeks late getting my period."

He ran two lights in Nyack, after he left the Grand Union parking lot. He had planned to buy Archie a birthday gift of some kind before he returned to the clinic, and automatically he headed toward the shopping center on the outskirts of Nyack. But he could not think of anything now except what Penny had just told him. He wondered if he was going to have to pull over and vomit, and he thought of just putting his foot all the way to the floor on the gas pedal and letting the Volkswagen smash into the truck ahead of him.

Tears stung his eyes. His mind was tortured with the certain notion that it could not be true and could not be happening to him, and yet it was true, it had happened, and for the first time since that Wednesday night when he had put Margaret into the ground the way someone would bury a dog, the enormity of what he had done hit him full force.

At the shopping center he pulled into an empty space, cut the ignition, and sat there holding himself like a small boy with a bellyache. His hands shook so that he could not light a cigarette, and he threw the last cigarette in his package away.

What he needed was a drink.

He got out of the car and walked aimlessly up toward the road, looking for a bar. There was no bar nearby; he knew it, and he retraced his steps, wondering if he could still drive. His knees seemed to want to give, and he coughed back what came out like a sudden sob.

A drink, or he would just let go everything.

Then he remembered that there was a bar in the bowling alley next to the A&P.

Inside, Neal ordered himself a double Jack Daniels. He drank it in one gulp, caught his breath, and directed the bartender to pour another.

—I don't believe in abortion, Neal. It's taking a life.

—What about Margaret's life?

—That was an accident!

—And if you're pregnant, what's that?

The whiskey began to restore him. He was able to remember the times Margaret's period had come late and it hadn't meant anything.

He gave himself back all the rules for staving off panic which he had presented to his patients at the clinic.

Number One: Get your bearings; where are you?

He heard the thunder of the bowling balls streaking down to clatter against the pins.

He heard the noise of the jukebox and recognized The Doors singing "Hello, I love you, won't you tell me your name?"

The bartender set the second drink before him.

He started to pick it up when he saw a familiar face.

It was Linda Chayka, the waitress from the diner where he stopped some mornings for breakfast. She was a dumpy brunette in a tight sweater, the sort who managed to work sex into a simple hello at seven in the morning.

She waved at Neal and Neal waved back.

She looked as though she were going to join him.

Finish the drink and leave.

He couldn't do it all at once as he had with the first one. He took a breath, and while he waited to have the second gulp, Linda Chayka began walking toward him. Her breasts bobbed under her orange sweater; a man at the other end of the bar gave a low whistle and she blushed with gratitude.

Neal tossed down the rest of the whiskey and slapped four dollars down on the bar.

"Hello, Dr. Dana."

"Hi, Linda."

"What's your hurry?"

"I have to get back to work."

He gave her a little two-fingered salute of farewell, noticing as he did the very ample bosom Linda had thrust near his coat. "So long." He smiled, noticing the gold pin attached to her orange sweater, a Zodiac pin identical to the one Margaret had been buried wearing.

Was it an illusion, his mind playing tricks?

He pushed through the door, out into the fresh air.

Was that to be the next step in this deadly game: fanciful reminders of Margaret?

But the whiskey said calmly, why wouldn't two women from the same town buy the same kind of pin?

Astrology was in, wasn't it?

Wasn't that fact the reason for all of it?

CHAPTER 14

Tiffany, the Siamese, sat on Neal's lap and watched the bubbles in Neal's glass of champagne with calculating crossed eyes.

Archie Gamble and Neal were comparing notes on their childhood.

Before coming here, Neal had stopped at the police precinct on River Road and reported Margaret's "disappearance" to Tom Baird. The officer had taken down the pertinent information, but Neal had been surprised by the faint smile on Tom's face. Neal and Margaret had never known the policeman well, but he had stopped by their house on a few occasions and had drinks with them, while he warned them against burning anything outdoors during dry spells or questioned them about hunters who poached in the woods.

What had moved him to smile? Had he decided that Margaret had left Neal after an inconsequential family squabble, or was he one of those people who suffered from "pathognomic parapraxis"—an inability to keep a straight face upon hearing of someone else's misfortune?

He *had* smiled. Neal mulled it over in his mind as Archie Gamble described his father's tyranny. Neal half-listened and

116

thought vaguely of his own father. He had hated him every bit as much as Archie claimed to despise his, but the tyranny was of a different sort, the worst kind: the tyranny of the weak. Norman Dana had been a big, muscular, table-pounding job-jumper whose rages were invariably followed by self-pitying tears and meaningless wails of *mea culpa*. He would actually get down on his knees and weep into his wife's lap; Neal's mother treated him like a little boy she had always to forgive for being naughty.

Neal had to force himself to keep up his end of the conversation.

He said, "I was terrible at all sports. I loved long-hair music; my friends were bespectacled library-goers, and my father had a habit of calling me 'Cornelia.'" (—Son, will you forgive Daddy for that? Oh, Daddy's so bad!)

"My girlhood wasn't much different," Archie chuckled. "I always had my nose in a book, hated football and baseball, and loved opera. *My* old man once said he wouldn't hit me because he didn't hit girls."

Neal and Archie laughed and so did Mrs. Muckermann. Dru was in the kitchen slamming dishes around furiously, still in a fit over Anna Muckermann's surprise visit. A friend on her way to Tarrytown had deposited Mrs. Muckermann on the Gambles' doorstep in Piermont. Dru had no alternative but to ask her to join the birthday party. Mrs. Muckermann had remembered that they had decided to have the party on Saturday night instead of the following Tuesday, which was the actual birthday, so she had arrived with gift-wrapped presents for both Archie and Neal.

Mrs. Muckermann said, "You *see?* You *are* typical time twins; you have a great deal in common! And you're both typical Geminis with Taurus rising."

Archie said, "Hi there, TV viewers. I want you to meet my athtro-twin. Ithn't he marvy? As boys, we were thimply thick-ening thissies!"

"The interest in music, of course, is the Taurine influence," said Mrs. Muckermann.

"That's right," Archie said. "That famous pianist, Harry Truman, is a Taurus."

Mrs. Muckermann regarded him with cold eyes. "Brahms was a Taurus," said she, "and Sullivan of Gilbert and Sullivan, Nellie Melba, and Irving Berlin. Fred Astaire, Bing Crosby, and Perry Como are all Taureans, too."

"So is that distinguished politician, Shirley Temple," Archie added, getting up to pour more Piper.

Had Tom Baird somehow heard the reason for Margaret's absence three years ago? It was unlikely; everyone but Neal's close friends had thought she was in Bucks County looking after her mother, who was convalescing from an illness.

Since Margaret's death, Neal had often found himself wondering how life would have seemed to him if it were really true that Margaret had simply disappeared. Cold. Populated with the likes of a Cliff Bates who hadn't even bothered to discuss it at length with Neal or to ask Neal to come to brunch anyway, and with a police officer who smiled . . . *smiled* when Neal announced he had no clue to Margaret's possible whereabouts. And the Gambles? Neal had told them over the telephone last night that he was going to the police. Archie had all but dismissed the subject, murmuring something about such things happening "to the best of us."

How could the Gambles presume to know what had happened between Neal and Margaret? Did they imagine that Margaret would actually run off without a word over a silly argument concerning the show?

All of it was such an injustice to Margaret! She had deserved better than that! She had been such a good woman, trying eternally to improve herself, going to so much trouble every day to make life gracious, meaningful. God, and to have it be someone like Penny Bissel who would strike her down— Neal was convinced of that now; Margaret had not hit Penny.

It was Margaret who had been unable to finish what she was saying: "Face what you are! Cheap, CHE—"

Yes. Cheap!

How could he not have seen that from the beginning? How could he have missed the way Penny began every sentence with "Like," the way she picked at hangnails and let her tongue root around her teeth to wipe away food particles when she finished eating, the way she left the bathroom door open when she was on the toilet, the way she pinned a ripped seam in a dress instead of sewing it, and her habit of combing her hair constantly: on the street, in restaurants, even immediately after lovemaking—her perpetual fixation with her hair, and that particularly stupid expression which came over her face as she jerked the comb up and down, like someone priming a pump.

And now Penny was two weeks late . . . now there was a very good possibility that she was carrying Neal Dana's child. Carrying a motive for Neal Dana's murder of his wife.

"Your lack of interest in sports is consistent with the Taurine inertia," Mrs. Muckermann was saying as she unwrapped a stick of Juicy Fruit. "Taurus is a slow, bovine sign; Taurean children are often dreamers. Introspective. I can see where the males might be considered slightly sissified as youngsters. Rudolph Valentino was a Taurus. Henry Fonda is. Tyrone Power was, and James Mason is."

"Freud was, too," Archie Gamble said. "But Neal and I are Geminis, remember?"

"Geminis with *Taurus rising*," said Mrs. Muckermann, popping the gum into her mouth. "Taurus is a decided influence."

Neal glanced down at the cat hairs accumulating on his brown slacks and pushed Tiffany off his lap. Margaret had never liked cats after she had seen one kill a baby sparrow . . . Neal didn't see how he could give Sinister away. He sat there remembering the way Margaret had put all her maternal energies into looking after the bird. He wretchedly recalled his inertia over their vague plans for looking into the possibility of adopting a child. It hadn't been Margaret's idea, it had been Neal's, and she hadn't pushed it, but why hadn't he been sensitive enough to her needs to encourage it? What kind of barren, ungratifying existence had he forced on her? How bravely and thoughtfully she had tried to make the best of it! And he had dared to cross off her interest in subjects like astrology as hogwash, just as though Neal Dana knew wiser ways to come to grips with the monotony of life.

The champagne was reaching him; he called out in his mind for Margaret to forgive him, and guiltily he envisioned her there with him, enjoying this discussion of astrology, punishing himself with the knowledge of how it would please her.

As though she were reading his mind, Mrs. Muckermann inquired, "What sign is your wife, Neal?"

"Virgo."

"Yes, well, the Taurean side of your nature probably doesn't like the critical character of Virgo . . . but Gemini is ruled by Mercury, as Virgo is: you both enjoy people; you're both outgoing. Of course, Virgo's a little more realistic." Then she said, "Has Archie shown you his chart and explained it to you? The same things would apply to you, of course."

"I've been sparing him that," said Archie.

"You really should look at it," Mrs. Muckermann told Neal. "King Lear once remarked, 'The stars above govern our conditions.'"

Archie said, "He made that remark to Shakespeare, didn't he?"

She ignored the sarcasm and continued. "But I favor a philosophy that believes we can work *with* our stars to change our conditions."

"The fool is ruled by his stars, the wise man rules his stars, is that it?" Neal said.

Mrs. Muckermann said flatly, "No . . . You never rule your

stars, my dear Neal: you work with your stars. And you *must* know what to be wary of, what aspects to watch, good and bad."

Archie was rolling his eyes back in his head, and holding his palms up in his lap in a "what do you do?" gesture.

"Oh, I know Archie's making faces behind my back," Mrs. Muckermann said, "and since you're his astro-twin, Neal, you're probably highly skeptical, too, but it's for your own good that I warn you."

"Warn me?" Neal said.

"You're very badly aspected right now."

But it was not until Dru had served the moules marinières, French rolls, and romaine and onion salad, that Mrs. Muckermann really got rolling. She was drinking champagne with the meal as fast as Archie could pour it, and she was monopolizing the conversation, leaving no doubt in anyone's mind that Saturn's malignant influence was "probably already" affecting Neal's and Archie's lives. She dragged in the moon-Mars square again, rode hard on all the oppositions being stimulated, and paused only long enough to advise Dru that she had not chopped the garlic for the moules fine enough.

"I just swallowed quite a sliver of it," she cackled. "You'll all pay tomorrow."

Dru began kicking Archie violently under the table at that point, and when she went into the kitchen for more rolls, she called to Archie, "Can you come here a moment, darling? I need help with something."

Archie gave Neal an apologetic smile and left him with Anna Awful.

Dru said, "She is *not* staying overnight!"

"I agree. Where's the bus schedule?"

"On the counter. Does she think she's invited for the weekend, Archie?" Dru said incredulously.

"It sounds like it. We'll all pay tomorrow—what does that

mean if it doesn't mean she's planning to see us at breakfast?"

"And get her *off* Neal's back, Archie! I don't think her little gifts for you two were the least bit amusing!"

Both Neal and Archie had received a copy of *4000 Names for Your Baby.*

"She wasn't trying to amuse us," Archie said. "It's all that business about Mars, Neptune and Leo being in the House of Offspring. You know she can't let go of anything; she keeps harping away on the same damn things! And she's crocked, you realize?"

"Pissed! Did you see Neal's face when he unwrapped it?"

"The poor bastard just left the police!" Archie said. "And I'm damn sure he suspects Margaret's left him for this Tuto."

"I don't know, Archie. I think he'd be angrier. He just looks all shook up."

Archie was running his finger down the bus listings. He said, "Anna Awful is the crowning blow, regardless of what he thinks! First she tells him there'll be violent upheavals in his life, then she tells him it's all right, though, because Mars, Neptune and Leo are going to provide progeny! She never stops to think that somebody might not want progeny!"

Dru sighed. "I know. Thank God he doesn't have any interest in it; if he believed her, he'd have a perfect excuse for going out and hanging himself!"

"So would I."

"So would you . . . Did you hear her tell him what his first name meant?"

Archie said, "Even if he doesn't have any interest in it, it can begin to get you. Enough of it can begin to get you . . . What about his first name?"

Dru dropped more rolls into the bread basket. "While you were up in the bathroom she picked up the baby-name book and said, 'Cornelius means battle horn, and you'll be doing a lot of battling in the days to come.' "

"What'd he say?"

"He didn't even smile. He just looked at her and he said, 'I hope my horn helps me, then. Or am I beyond help?'"

"Naturally she assured him he was beyond help, right?" Archie said.

"Just about. Oh, she's a bitch on wheels, Arch! Do you know she came out here before dinner and she had the nerve to tell me I was playing right into Saturn's hands by not having a cake for your birthday!"

"Did you tell her that I don't like cake?" Archie said. He passed her the bus schedule. "Here's one leaving at ten-something. I don't have my glasses. What is it, ten-twenty or ten-thirty?"

"Ten-twenty . . . No, I didn't tell her you don't like cake! Why should I defend myself? She said, 'Oh, sweetie, now's a time you have to work at your marriage! Archie's marital aspects are very turbulent!' I almost told her I didn't have a marriage in the ninth place!"

Archie said, "One word about that business tonight and I'll get on the ten-twenty with her."

"You ought to rescue Neal now . . . Archie?"

"What?"

She touched his lips with her fingers. "You said it can begin to get you. It isn't getting *you*, is it?"

"I wouldn't miss her if she fell through an open manhole tomorrow," he said.

"But it isn't getting you, is it? You don't believe in any of it, do you?"

"You know better than that."

She said, "Because it *is* spooky. All this bit about bad marital aspects and Liddy turning up with that news about your divorce being illegal, and Margaret—"

He leaned down and kissed her. "Hush . . . How'm I going to get her on the bus in an hour and forty minutes? What'll I tell her?"

"First get that glass out of her hand, or she'll pass out," said

Dru. "I'm bringing in coffee *before* I serve the mousse."

"But what'll I say? It's heave-ho time, Mrs. Muckermann!"

Dru said, "Tell her the sun is shining on her House of Departure."

They giggled, and Archie said, "We're going to have to put you out on Uranus, Mrs. Muckermann."

Dru held her stomach, laughing. "Put on your shoes, Mrs. Muckermann, your Capricorn's going traveling."

Archie snapped his fingers. "*I* know," he said. "I'll get Neal to say one of his colleagues is giving him a birthday party later tonight, and we're expected. I'll just tell the old witch we're going to drop her at the bus stop on the way."

Anna Muckermann said, "That won't be necessary, Archie." She stood in the doorway carrying her empty champagne glass.

"Your other guest," she said in a brittle voice, "has just gone upstairs to be ill. As for me, I'm prepared to leave immediately."

CHAPTER 15

Visions of unpaid bills and a dwindling savings account danced sadistically through Archie Gamble's head.

Tiffany's owners, the Cages, had given him permission to drive their Buick until his car was repaired. Tiffany liked to stow away under the front seat, and it was to her that Archie addressed himself after depositing Mrs. Muckermann at the bus stop on 9W.

"Well, we'll have to go out and kill a few bluebirds for our dinner now," he said. "We just lost our meal ticket, old girl."

Dru had insisted on driving Neal home in his Volkswagen, and Archie was to pick her up there. Neal had been pale and nauseated. While Mrs. Muckermann had sat outside smoldering in the Buick, waiting for Archie, Dru had told Archie, "I'm so worried about Neal!"

Archie slowed up for the turn off 9W.

He said, "The hell with me, right, Tiffany? First things first! She's worried about Neal!"

Archie made the turn and lit a True as he went down the hill toward Piermont.

*Damn* Dru! She should have wanted to lend *him* a little

support, never mind Neal Dana! Dru had gotten him involved in the whole Muckermann mess to begin with! If it hadn't been for Anna Muckermann and this idiotic show, which was now *kaput* where Archie Gamble was concerned, Archie could have knocked off several articles and had a novel in the works.

The ride with Mrs. Muckermann to the bus stop had been undergone in stony silence. The only thing Mrs. Muckermann had said, before she got out of the car, was: "Our association is terminated. I have no doubt you'll let Saturn carry you along the rest of the way on your self-destructive path. I feel sorry for you, Archie Gamble. There's more trouble ahead."

All right, it was a lot of crap, but it *could* get to you!

"It isn't getting to *you*, is it?" Dru had asked, as though she had sensed that it was beginning to; then she had turned right around and chosen to look after Neal, left Archie to cope with Mrs. Muckermann, and now drive back by himself with his nerves in knots!

Archie could feel his drinks. He went along River Road slowly, telling himself all Mrs. Muckermann would need now would be the satisfaction of Archie's destroying himself in an automobile wreck. He laughed, envisioning a newspaper report of the wreck as Mrs. Muckermann would write it. The driver was not intoxicated; he was badly aspected.

But the smile passed from his face. Better men than Archie Gamble had become wary of astrological omens: FDR, for one. He had consulted the famous astrologer Louis de Wohl; there were stories told that he had changed the date of the Presidential Inaugural to January 20 from March 4 in a futile effort at upsetting the pattern of American president's dying during the Jupiter-Saturn conjunction. Nehru was a stanch believer in astrology; Aldous Huxley, Henry Miller, Ralph Waldo Emerson; Benjamin Franklin, Goethe, and Mark Twain, who had said, "I was born with Haley's Comet, and I expect to die upon its return"—and did . . . Teddy Roosevelt had mounted his horoscope on a chess board which always stood on a table in the White House.

The hell with it—his drinks were doing his thinking!

He slowed up near Neal's hill. There was a car blocking the entrance, and Archie missed the turn. He had to back up, and as he did, the other car went forward. It was a black Ford Falcon; the street light caught the reflection of a small, shiny penny fixed to the door.

Archie braked the Buick and watched the car go down River Road. A woman was driving. He had not been able to see her face, only the bright green scarf she wore around her head.

Margaret Dana?

Tiffany took a swipe at the cuff on Archie's trousers.

"Okay! Okay!" Archie complained. "We're going."


Dru didn't want to go.

"We can't just leave him, Arch. He feels *awful!*"

Archie decided to tell her about seeing the Falcon after he got her home. If it had been Margaret Dana, she had not made an appearance.

Archie said, "How do you think *I* feel?"

"Don't always think of yourself, Archie! You have me; he doesn't have anyone!"

"I have her, folks. That's why I took Mrs. Muckermann to the bus alone."

"What'd she say, Archie?"

"Next time come along and find out."

"Archie, Neal is heartsick!"

"He's just got a load on."

"Like you," she said. "Only champagne doesn't make him mean."

"Now I'm mean. I just lost the show, thousands of dollars down the drain, and—"

She slammed a coffee mug down on the kitchen table. "The show! Money! Is that all you care about? Neal's in there with all the sawdust spilling out of him!"

The old rag doll analogy! She had used it time and again

when Archie was torching over Liddy, in the beginning days of his relationship with Dru.

"So that's it," Archie said.

"*What's* it?"

"You've found a new rag doll to mend! A little psychologist doll this time, instead of a little writer doll. Jesus!"

"You just can't stand it if you're not the center of attraction!"

"Oh, he's in for a treat!" He imitated Dru's voice saying the things she had said when they were first sleeping together. " 'Am I as good as she was in bed?' . . . 'Would you rather be with her?' . . . 'Did you think of her while you were touching me?' . . . 'My breasts aren't very big, are they?' "

Dru's eyes flashed. "You just lay off my breasts!"

" 'Neal?' " he continued, imitating her whine. " 'Do you mind it that I'm so small?' "

"Liddy's breasts are like goddamn hanging hams!" Dru said.

"Hear that in there, Neal?" said Archie. "Miss Ping-Pong Balls doesn't like Miss Hanging Hams."

"That did it!" said Dru.

"Oh, look," Archie said, reaching for her. "I didn't mean it, love. I'm just upset about—"

She pushed him away and regarded him with an icy expression. "Don't touch me," she said quietly, emphatically. "Go!"

"I'll say good night to Neal and meet you in the car," he said.

She said, "I'm not ready to leave yet."

"Well, *I* am!"

"Leave. I don't care what you do."

"Leave without you?"

"I'm not helpless. I'll get home."

"That's not the point!"

"Oh? Was there a point?"

"Dru, I've just lost my whole summer's work! That's the *point!* How do you think I *feel?*"

She said, "You're not really heartsick. You've just got a load on."

"Okay, he's heartsick! He didn't puke up liquor; he puked up his goddamn heart!"

"*Low*-wer your voice, Archie."

"Are you coming with me? Now?"

"No."

"Happy Birthday to you, too," Archie said.

She was busy making coffee with her back turned to him.

He said, "Are you coming with me now?"

"Does it look that way?" She was counting the tablespoons of coffee under her breath as she put them into the pot.

"If you stay here," Archie said, "you won't find me there when you finally decide to go home!"

"Promises, promises," she said coldly.

"I mean it, Dru!"

". . . four, five, six," she said, "and one for the pot."

He kicked the kitchen door open with his foot and stamped into the living room. Neal Dana had gone back upstairs to the bathroom; Archie could hear the repeated flushing of the toilet.

Archie went outside and stood on the porch.

It was a beautiful moonlit night, and the sight of the enormous full moon positioned over the Hudson made him feel all the more sorry for himself. You could see this very same view from the Cages' bedroom, and that was where Dru and he should be now; that was what he needed now.

Then he had a ridiculous thought: the moon ruled Cancer; the moon ruled Dru. And he remembered that poem Mrs. Muckermann used to recite:

> Who changes like a changeful season,
> Holds fast and lets go without reason?
> Who is there can give adhesion
> To Cancer?

As he lit a cigarette, he looked inside and saw Dru setting out a cream pitcher and a sugar bowl on the living-room table.

Yes, the good little mother preparing to put the sawdust back in the rag doll. The *new* rag doll.

"*Cherchez la mère*," as Mrs. Muckermann had often remarked, "*et vous trouverez le Cancer!*"

He pushed open the screen door and walked across the lawn to the Buick.

After he started the motor, he waited briefly; then he backed up the car and put his foot on the brake. He could see her through the window. Dru was arranging the coffee mugs on the table now, oblivious to what was taking place out in the driveway.

Archie reached down and pulled Tiffany out from under the seat.

"Come on," he said, "you don't want to go all the way to New York," and he dropped the cat out the window before taking off.


About forty-five minutes after Archie Gamble left, Dru left, too, taking the Volkswagen as Neal told her to do.

Sobered up and over-coffeed, Neal knew he wouldn't sleep for a while. He went across and opened a window, then put on *The Pajama Game*, smoking a cigarette and lying on the couch as he listened to Eddie Foy, Jr., and the ensemble sing "Racing with the Clock."

May, 1954.

He remembered the night Margaret and he had seen the show, because the same day the Senate had defeated a proposed constitutional amendment extending the vote to eighteen-year-olds. It had depressed Margaret; she had been a part of a Rockland County committee which had worked to try to have the amendment passed. They had talked about it at supper in the Algonquin after the show. He had always been so proud of Margaret because she cared about such things. He had always compared her with Cliff Bates' wife, a rattle-brained woman who had stopped reading the newspapers when the *Journal-American* folded, with Cholly Knickerbocker's column no longer available. Her conversations were laced with first names of people she had never met, like "Jackie" and "Cee-Zee," and "Chessy" and "Ba." She dressed like a page out of *Seventeen*, and called busboys and parking lot attendants and ushers "dawdling," winking at them like some glamorous movie actress patronizing the little people.

Margaret had had such class.

Neal could not remember her ever having embarrassed him.

He had not deserved Margaret. He lay there remembering so many things about her, so many of her ways, and his eyes brimmed with tears when Janis Page began to sing, "I'm Not at All in Love."

Margaret never would have left him as Dru Gamble had left Archie tonight to drive Neal home; she never would have let Neal leave without her. Neal had appreciated all that Dru had done—my God what would he have done without her?—but he could not help thinking that Margaret would not have done it for anyone, much less a relative stranger, leaving Neal to fend for himself. Margaret had always put Neal first.

Then that damn baby-name book Mrs. Muckermann had presented to Neal—Neal remembered the swift punch he had felt to his bowels as he took off the wrapping and saw the title! It was then that he had begun to fall apart at the seams —to imagine, with the help of all the champagne, that the Fates, the stars, whatever name you wanted to call them by, were conspiring against him, moving in now for the kill. What perfect irony, too, that it would be astrology and an astrologer that would unnerve him; poetic justice for Margaret!

As Eddie Foy, Jr., and Reta Shaw began "I'll Never be Jealous Again," Neal got up and carried the coffee cups into the kitchen. He could not allow himself to lie around remembering things; it was a time when he must discipline his mind, keep it occupied. He had papers to read: one on "Crying at the Happy Ending" in a back issue of a professional journal, and one on blushing from another quarterly. Next week he would lunch with the Doubleday editor; he would set his mind to preparations for that.

Penny had promised to take the quinine pills as Neal had directed; they could do nothing for her if she were pregnant, but they might induce her period if she were not. He put the cream pitcher in the refrigerator, slamming the door shut so that it shook the house with its force as he thought again of his foolishness in trusting Penny to do anything. If she had been responsible in the first place, if she had taken the other pills as she claimed she had, there would be no reason for alarm now!

As he began to rinse out the coffee mugs, he heard Sinister shouting in the living room. The old bird had finally come to! Neal had begun to fear that Sinister had sunk into a deep depression over Margaret's absence. For days the parrot had been reluctant to sing or speak Italian, or say much more than "I'm Sinister. I love the view," in a pathetic, melancholy tone.

Sinister was making up for it now!

Neal turned off the water to listen. The bird was really going at it. Neal smiled and went across to the refrigerator to get out the jar of worms. He supposed he was overfeeding the parrot; he would call Dr. Halliday, Monday, and check the diet. He was definitely not going to get rid of the bird; keeping him was the least he could do. He had to admit that he had even grown fond of Sinister.

He walked into the living room in time to see Tiffany Cage leap through the window carrying Sinister by the neck.

He heard a voice behind him cry, "I tried to stop her, but she was too fast for me! She was already at him when I came in the door!"

Neal turned around and faced Forrest Bissel.

CHAPTER 16

It was too late for Sinister; Tiffany had run to the woods with him.

As Neal and Forrest returned to the living room, Neal put the flashlight on his desk, and turned off *Pajama Game.*

"Are you in trouble, Forrest?"

"I don't know."

"What do you mean you don't know?"

"I just don't know." He sat down on the hassock and chewed on his knuckles. He had let his wheat-colored hair grow long; he had sideburns now, too. Neal had not seen him in months, but the morose, repentant expression in his hazel eyes was familiar. Forrest was wearing white sneakers, soiled white ducks, and a T-shirt under a cotton Madras zip-front jacket. Neal noticed the bulge in the left pocket of the jacket.

"If you're not in trouble, why are you carrying a gun?"

"The dog," Forrest answered.

"What dog?"

"Kendal."

"What do you know about Kendal?"

"What do I know about her? He lives next door and she's a Doberman. They can kill, Dobermans."

Neal said, "I mean *how* do you know about her?" Neal sat down on the couch facing Forrest, with the coffee table between them.

"It's a long story, Dr. Dana. I don't know how to tell you."

Neal said, "You haven't been prowling around the Nickersons' place, have you, Forrest?"

"No. But they think I have."

"If you haven't, how would they even know you?"

"They've seen me."

"Where?"

"Up here," he said. He gave a nervous little cough and stared at the floor.

"Up *here*? You haven't been up here before."

"Yes, I have."

"You've been up here?"

"Yes, Dr. Dana. A lot of times."

"When? *Why?*"

"A lot of times. To see Marg."

"Who?"

"Marg. Mrs. Dana."

"What are you talking about, Forrest? You're not making any sense."

"I got to know Mrs. Dana."

"What do you mean you got to know her?"

"You know. *That* way."

Neal snapped, "Have you been drinking?"

"It was me who gave her Sinister."

"You sold Sinister to her? She never said—"

"I gave her Sinister. I taught him the Christmas carols. I gave him to her for Christmas."

"You gave Sinister to Mrs. Dana? Why?"

"For Christmas." He shrugged. "I was going with her."

"What kind of a joke is this? What have you and Penny decided to—"

Forrest didn't let him finish. "No," he said. "My sister doesn't know anything about it. No one does."

Neal got up and walked across the room to get his pack of Trues. "You'd better start making sense, Forrest. You're not making sense."

He heard Forrest drop something on the coffee table, turned around, and saw the revolver.

Forrest said, "If you want to shoot me, shoot me."

"I don't want to shoot you," said Neal. "I want you to try and think straight."

"We were lovers, Dr. Dana."

Neal could not suppress a tone of amusement. "You and my wife?"

"Yes. We couldn't help ourselves."

Neal went over and sat down again on the couch. He lit a True and offered one to Forrest. Forrest refused. He heaved a sigh and would not look at Neal.

Neal said, "Now, Forrest, listen. You're very confused. I want to help you. But I think it's better if you get a good night's sleep. I think you should drive over to the clinic with me and—"

"She has a wart on her stomach."

"What?"

"Doesn't she? Near her belly button there's a wart the size of a dime. She's always talking about getting it removed."

Neal didn't say anything.

Forrest Bissel said, "I gave her the parrot and she named him Sinister, because I'm left-handed and left-handed aspects in astrology are called Sinister."

"Go on," Neal said softly.

"I'm not nuts and I'm not going to the clinic, so I better get everything off my chest."

"Yes, that's best."

"I came here or we went up to the Shady Rest Motel near Fishkill."

Neal remembered the nightie and the bathing suit he had found in the Pan Am bag.

Forrest said, "I wasn't the one that started things."

One night, weeks ago, Margaret had remarked that she had seen Forrest in Piermont . . . that Forrest was a Scorpio.

"But I fell for her like a ton of bricks, I'll say that." Then he said, "You believe me now, don't you?"

Neal nodded.

"I won't blame you if you hit me," Forrest said. "You probably feel like punching my face in."

"What for?"

"What *for?*" He looked at Neal for the first time since he had started talking. "For taking your wife away! You still think I'm nuts or something? We were going on a camping trip! She was trying to get you involved in some kind of astrology show so we could have more nights together! We had Wednesday nights because she told you she took Italian lessons! I was going with Marg right under your nose!"

Neal said, "If I punched your face in, what good would it do?"

"If *you'd* done it to *my* woman, I'd punch yours in."

"Well, that's unlikely."

"We were going on a camping trip, but I started getting chicken."

"Why?"

"You know me, Dr. Dana. I don't have any stick-to-it-ive-ness. I mean, that's a lack. I lack that. And there was a big age difference. When Marg's fifty, I'll only be thirty-two. You know what I mean?"

"Yes."

"Then they started letting Kendal out and I got afraid to come here. Dobermans kill."

"So you said."

"And it began to wear off. How I felt. I still really respect her, but . . . you know?"

"Ummm hmmm."

"And that's why I'm worried, because I wouldn't want anything to happen to her."

"What do you think could happen to her?"

"I know she's gone. I've been trying to call her."

"But you got *me*. So you didn't say anything."

"That was me calling. I was worried. Then I heard you reported her missing. That's why I came here."

"Why?"

"I think she might have done something to herself. She really has a case on me."

"I see."

"She really wanted to go on that camping trip, and I told her I didn't want to go."

"What did she say?"

"She said I owed it to her."

"I see . . . Who told you I reported that she was missing, Forrest?"

"Officer Baird told me."

"Why would he tell you?"

"One time he saw us together. It was a Wednesday night and we were parked down by the river in Nyack."

"In the Volkswagen?"

"Yes. He knew what was going on. He could tell. So yesterday I had an occasion to see him. A little trouble came up about something else. He wanted to talk to me about it, and it was then he asked me if *I* knew anything about Marg's disappearance."

"What did you tell him?"

Forrest shrugged. "I said I didn't. I wasn't going to tell him I was afraid she might have done something to herself. I figured it was my duty to come here and tell you that."

"I see." Neal stubbed out his cigarette and said, "Where had you planned to go camping?"

"Some woods."

"I see."

"We hadn't doped it out yet."

"I see."

"I wish you'd stop saying you see. I feel lousy that you're so nice about it, Dr. Dana . . . I'm not any good at all, I guess. I'm just not any good at all. I'm beginning to see that. I screw up everything. I wish you'd punch me in the mouth. That's what I deserve."

"No," said Neal. "No."

"You're a right guy, you know that? I've failed you more ways than one, more ways than you know, but you're always on my side. I meant it, too, when I said I didn't start anything with Marg. She threw herself in my path, you know what I mean?"

"Ummm hmmm."

"I mean, Marg fell for me like a ton of bricks."

"I thought you fell for her that way?"

"I mean, I was impressed—a woman like her going after me. But like I said, there's a big age difference. And to level with you, Dr. Dana, I need more than she can give me that way. Do you see my point?"

"Yes."

"I'm a Scorpio, if you know what that means," he said, smiling shyly.

"I'll tell you one thing, though, Forrest."

"What's that, Dr. Dana?"

"You ought to go with Margaret to the woods," he said. "You do owe it to her; she's right." Then he picked up the revolver and pumped three bullets through Forrest Bissel's heart.

After he had cleaned things up, Neal went upstairs to find the blue Vycron polyester Slumber Bag.

By four-thirty A.M., Forrest was buried beside "Marg."

CHAPTER 17

When Druscilla Gamble arrived back at the Cages', she found a florist's box on the back porch. It was addressed to Mr. Archie Gamble. It contained two dozen purple and red anemones with a card: "Happy Birthday and love, Liddy." Scribbled across the top of the box was, "Sorry these are late; I didn't know you were staying at the Cages.' Galen Florists, Nyack."

Archie had made good his promise not to be there. Dru turned on the lights in the living room and turned them off again as soon as she saw the dirty dinner plates and champagne glasses and the overflowing ashtrays. She was certainly not going to stand at the kitchen sink and do a million dishes while Archie was on his way to the arms of Liddy.

Arms? Boobs was more like it. Again she felt the sting of his dirty crack about Miss Ping-Pong Balls. But she was more depressed than angry now. It was her own fault that Archie had gone to New York. She had no doubt that was where he had headed. It was her own fault, and then again maybe the whole mess wasn't anyone's fault; who was Druscilla Gamble to say the stars weren't to blame?

139

"It can begin to get you," Archie had said earlier that evening. "Enough of it can begin to get you."

She had said, "It isn't getting *you*, is it?"

What had he answered? She had forgotten.

The champagne had reached her, too, but like all the other times when she had become quite drunk without any noticeable change in her facade, she hadn't realized it until later. She could see it now: babying Neal Dana that way—Archie was right, she had found a new little rag doll to mend. Alcohol always affected her that way. One of the worst fights she and Archie had ever had occurred during a telethon which was raising money for a children's hospital. They had stayed up late to watch Tim Hardin appear on the show and sing "Don't Make Promises," one of their favorite records, and they had made a batch of stingers to keep them company. About two hours and three stingers into the show, Dru had gone to the telephone, called in and pledged one hundred dollars. It was during the early days of their marriage, when Archie's analysis was eating up all their money; he had shouted at her that they couldn't afford ten dollars, nevermind a hundred, but Dru had gone right on dialing, and soon the announcer was thanking Mr. and Mrs. Archie Gamble for their generous contribution.

"Boy, I hope our creditors are listening!" Archie had ranted, and Dru had sat there in tears, telling him he didn't care how many little children died, he only cared about Archie Gamble.

The next day she had given up stingers forever, a pledge she had actually kept for a year.

Dru went to the kitchen door and called Tiffany. When the cat didn't answer, she left the window open for her, then turned off the downstairs lights and went up to the bedroom.

She thought of calling the apartment in New York to see if Archie was there, and to apologize, but she didn't want to take the chance of finding out for certain that he wasn't there.

For a while, after she put on her nightie, she sat at Archie's desk and looked through *An Interpretation of Gemini*, written by an astrologer called Zodiack, whose style was gloomily familiar.

GEMINI—May 21–June 21

The third sign of the Zodiac, the twins.

Its symbol (II) represents the duality of good and evil and the unremitting conflict between contradictory mental processes.

Gemini is an air sign as are Libra and Aquarius.

Air stands for Intelligence, and because Gemini is ruled by the planet Mercury, the Gemini type is intellectual but fickle.

The Gemini is so often emotionally cold, he may use his mental gifts to deceive.

Because of his dual nature, he possesses the ability to live a double life.

The old saying "Easy come, easy go," applies to the Gemini. He squanders his energies in too many directions, squanders money, and tires quickly of the very "new things" he is always searching for.

The one thing you can always expect of the Gemini is something unexpected.

Dru turned the page to a "Compatibility Chart." She skipped down to

GEMINI AND CANCER

The insecure, overly-emotional Cancer may be too much for Gemini to cope with. This is the sign of motherly types who also make excellent teachers, but Gemini will not easily adapt to Cancer's "stay-at-home" personality. However, Cancer the crab has a hard shell and a tenacious nature, and may prove stronger than Gemini. Because Cancer is ruled by the moon, there is a great deal of intuition to assist in dealing with Gemini's deviousness. Not the best of combinations, but possible.

"Thanks a lot!" Dru said aloud.

Then she remembered that Liddy was a Scorpio, and her finger went down the column until she found GEMINI AND SCORPIO.

The scorpion is the only animal that can kill itself with the stinging instrument of its tail. Scorpio often seems to invite danger. It is the eighth sign, related to the eighth house, the House of Death. Intrepid, aggressive, erotic Scorpio may overwhelm Gemini in physical ways, but Gemini would always outwit him. An explosive combination!

Dru slammed the book shut. For a few moments she sat staring at the telephone; then she gave up, crawled into bed, put out the light and listened to Barry Farber on the radio until she fell asleep.

She was awakened by something dropping on her feet. She let out a shriek of terror as she sat up in bed clutching the sheet to her body.

"Who's there?"

She waited, and then she reached over and turned on the light.

She saw the limp body of Sinister, the blood from his mutilated black feathers staining the yellow-flowered sheets, and she began to scream.

Archie said, "It's all right now, love. It's all right."

"Thank God you're here! Oh, Arch, I've never been so afraid!"

"It was just a dead parrot."

"Just a dead parrot, folks. They're always dropping on me in my sleep."

"I thought you were being murdered," he said.

"Where were you?"

He said, "Right downstairs. I came in a few hours ago. You were asleep. I couldn't sleep." The truth was he hadn't wanted to, hadn't felt like sleeping. He had sat in the darkness of the living room chain-smoking, playing the radio softly.

She blew her nose and dropped the Kleenex into the wastebasket. Archie sat beside her on the bed with his arm around her waist.

She said, "Where's Tiffany now?"

"Out."

"I want to be sure and thank her for the gift. She shouldn't have gone to all that trouble."

"She's probably out getting something for me now."

"Probably. A nice bloody owl or something scrumptious like that . . . . Speaking of gifts, Arch."

He said, "I saw them. That was nice of Liddy."

"*Nice* of Liddy? Not unusual of Liddy, not strange of Liddy? She hasn't remembered your birthday in three years!"

"Dru, she hasn't been around for three years," he said.

"It's great having Dolly back where she belongs. I wonder if she'll send flowers on our anniversary?"

He changed the subject. "I shouldn't have put Tiffany out of the car," he said.

"Will you light me a cigarette? My hands are still shaking. . . . You were going to New York, weren't you?"

He reached in his shirt pocket for the pack of Trues. "I got all the way across the Tappan Zee bridge. Then I turned around in Tarrytown and came back. I went to Sbordone's for a few beers." At Tarrytown he had pulled into the Hilton, where he had called Liddy in New York and reached her answering service instead. He hadn't left his name. He had driven back across the bridge wondering where she was, and with whom, in the same way he had when they were married.

He scratched a match and lighted cigarettes for Dru and himself.

She said, "Were you going in to see Liddy?"

"No. I was just going to our apartment. I came back because I didn't have the keys."

"Thanks a lot."

"You know what I mean," he said, passing her the cigarette. "I wasn't going in to see Liddy. I was going in to sleep at our place."

She said, "I better call Neal and tell him about Sinister."

"Dru, it's four o'clock."

"He said that bird was like Margaret's child. He's probably worried sick!"

"Why give him the bad news now?"

"It isn't fair to let him worry all night, Arch."

"He probably doesn't even know Sinister's gone."

"The bird must have screamed. And Neal's a light sleeper, remember? An insomniac, remember? He may even be looking for Sinister. I think I should call him, Archie."

"You know him better than I do."

"Whatever *that* means," she said testily. He wasn't sure himself what he had meant by the remark, whether or not he really did suspect her of an intimacy with Neal. Perhaps it was a projection of his own feelings where Liddy was concerned. He didn't feel like thinking about any of it, but it was all just under the surface and came out in this senseless sniping. If they didn't clear the air somehow, he knew, they were in for a real all-nighter.

She reached for the phone and dialed the number while Archie took the sheet with Sinister's blood on it and stuffed it into the bathroom hamper.

"No answer," she said when he came back into the bedroom. "I bet he's out looking for Sinister."

"Or he might be on a late date with Margaret," said Archie. "Can you take a little more excitement?" He kicked off his loafers and sat cross-legged beside her on the bed, putting an ashtray between them. "I saw Margaret Dana tonight."

"At Sbordone's? How did you know it was her?"

"Not at Sbordone's. After I dropped Mrs. Muckermann off, as I was going up to get you. She was parked down by the turn."

"How do you know it was her, Arch?"

"She was in the Falcon with the penny on the door."

"Alone or with Tuto?"

"She was alone. I didn't get a good look at her. She was

wearing a green scarf over her head. When I slowed up for the turn, she saw where I was headed and took off."

"Why didn't you tell me when we were talking in the kitchen?"

He said, "I wanted you to come home with me. I thought maybe you'd hang around if I told you. I didn't know you'd hang around anyway."

"I'm sorry, Arch."

"I'm sorry, too, for that crack about your breasts."

"That was hitting below the belt, Archie."

He chuckled, and she said, "*All right*—it was above the belt. It was dirty pool just the same."

"I know," he said gently. "I'm sorry."

She said, "Archie? I hate everything, don't you? The way we are with each other lately, and this thing with Neal and Margaret. What would she be doing there?"

He shook his head. "I don't know . . . Maybe she was coming back for her clothes. Maybe she drove up the hill, saw you inside, and changed her mind."

"Maybe she was coming back period."

"In Tuto's car?" Archie said.

"If it is his car . . . I wish we'd asked Neal about that Falcon."

"I wish we'd stayed out of the whole damn mess," Archie sighed. "We should have left the letters and the diary in that bag, and minded our own business!"

"Something's fishy, isn't it, Arch?"

"Yeah." He put out his cigarette and began unbuttoning his shirt.

"Because he doesn't seem concerned about where she is. He never wonders where she is. It's as though he knows where she is, and he can't do anything about it."

"I know."

"You know, Arch? He acts resigned . . . the way you were when Liddy was running around with everything in pants."

"Liddy didn't run around with everything in pants," he snapped, "and I was never resigned."

"You *still* aren't resigned, you mean."

"You can't have it both ways, Dru." He got up and took off his trousers. "If I'm still not resigned, how could I have acted resigned?"

"You used to talk about Liddy the same way Neal talks about Margaret, that's all . . . how wonderful she was, how much style she had, how she could do this and that so well, and all the while you knew she was out catting around."

The truth of what she said compelled him to shout. "Don't stretch for the parallel! We don't have to look for similarities between Neal and me any more! Mrs. Muckermann will see to that!"

Dru walked by him and got a fresh sheet from the linen closet in the hall. "He makes her sound so pure and righteous," she persisted. "You'd think she was the Virgin Mary." Was she as jealous now of Margaret as she had always been of Liddy?

Archie said, "You'd never catch Liddy swallowing a lot of garbage about astrology!"

"Of course not! Liddy's far too intellectual for that! Why, she's the darling of the literati, the dynamo of the drawing room, the conversationalists' conversationalist, is old boobs-brain Liddy!"

"Call her what you want," he said, "but you can't call her gullible!"

Dru walked back in the bedroom, threw the sheet at him, and he caught it. As he shook it open, damning the fact they had strayed back into the argument, Dru said, "Call her madam. The hookers' hooker—Liddy Denyven!"

Archie slapped the sheet to the floor in a gesture of futility and sat down naked on the bed. He lit a cigarette and sank his chin into his palm. "I've about had it, Dru," he said.

"So have I," she answered angrily. "You can sleep in here! I'm going to sleep—" and then she let out a long wail as her bare foot stepped in a spot of Sinister's blood on the rug.

She ran and flung herself against Archie.

After the bedroom light was out Dru said, "Archie?" reaching for his hand under the sheet.

"What?"

"I don't like it out here."

He turned toward her and put his arms around her. "You have to get used to the country," he said. "Cats go after birds, dogs go after cats, vivisectionists go after dogs, old ladies go after vivisectionists. It's survival of the fittest, honey."

The last time he had seen Liddy, she had said, "Archie, I can't see you in the country." He had misunderstood, remember? He had thought she meant that she wouldn't be able to see him if he moved away for the summer. Touched, he had looked at her for a long moment before she had restated the remark. "I can't see you living in suburbia." . . . Or had she done it purposefully, to tease?

Dru said, "I don't mean just the wildlife. I mean everything that's happened since we first drove out here. Our car was smashed; we haven't been getting along; the Liddy thing; you've lost the show; whatever's going on with Neal and his wife—it's all bad news. This is the worst birthday party you've ever had, too. I'm sorry, Arch."

"It wasn't your fault."

"He seems like bad luck, Archie."

"Neal?"

"Yes. Maybe he's the dark twin. You know? Dark and light and the duality of good and evil? I was reading something about that in that book by Zodiack."

Archie stroked her arm and pressed his lips against her neck, remembering the way he had sat in the car outside

Neal's house earlier that evening, watching Dru set out the coffee mugs for Neal and herself. "Look at it from Neal's point of view," he murmured. "We weren't exactly good luck to him. It's probably been his worst birthday, too."

He wondered if that were true.

CHAPTER 18

"Virgo, the virgin—don't you believe it!" Mrs. Muckermann laughed. "If she's a Virgo, she's nothing but a nymphomaniac. Your own wife was, wasn't she?"

"Not Margaret," he said, as Mrs. Muckermann backed him closer to the wall. She had Kendal attached to her stomach by an umbilical cord. Kendal snarled at Neal.

Mrs. Muckermann said, "I could name you names of men she knew that way."

"No. There was only Forrest."

Kendal bared her teeth, watching Neal intently.

"Come closer, Dr. Dana. I'll tell you who else saw the wart."

"Who? The dog won't let me—"

"Kendal won't hurt you."

Neal moved forward an inch.

Mrs. Muckermann said, "There was Cliff."

"Who?"

"Cliff——." The last name drifted out of hearing.

"Say it again."

"Cliff——."

"I can't hear you."

"Cliff —ger."

"I almost heard you. What?"

"Cliff Hanger," Mrs. Muckermann answered, and then Kendal lunged forward and sank her teeth into the flesh of Neal's ankle.


Neal's leg jerked and he woke up.

He lay there remembering slowly that this was Thursday, the day Penny was going for the results of her pregnancy test.

Then he remembered that he was to stop in and see Tom Baird on his way to the clinic. The policeman had called last night. There was something he wanted Neal to see, and something he wanted to discuss with Neal.

But what seemed even more important was the dream from which Neal had just awakened.

Ever since Saturday night, Cliff Bates had been much on Neal's mind. He kept remembering a morning years ago when Cliff had been there after staying overnight. Cliff had started to go into the bathroom while Margaret was taking a bath. At the time, Neal had thought Cliff was just too absent-minded to hear her running the water and to realize the bathroom door was shut.

—Hey, Cliff, wait a second.

—What?

—Margaret's in there.

—Oh? Oh. Sorry.

But just for a fraction of a second the expression on Cliff's face had seemed to ask why that made any difference, as though there would be nothing new about Cliff sharing a bathroom with Margaret.

Margaret and Cliff?

No, Neal couldn't believe that. It was even easier to believe Margaret and Forrest Bissel. Margaret had had symptoms of early menopause last winter; that could have thrown her way out of whack, could conceivably explain such erratic and erotic behavior. She had probably suffered a minor nervous break-down, with Neal too distracted by Penny and the Doubleday business, to perceive it . . . It wasn't like Margaret to be devious, irresponsible . . . certainly not promiscuous.

And yet . . .

Neal got out of bed and went in to shower.

He could not control the unconscious; it would be there to taunt him and stage its little black comedies in his dreams, but he could continue to discipline his conscious thoughts. He was not going to indulge his suspicions and fears, his guilt or his anger. He left off thinking of Margaret and the graves out in the woods with Slumber Bags in them. He concentrated on the smell of Dial soap and the hot shower water needling his back. He was aware of a choking sound the toilet made as he flushed it—he had never noticed that before—and a certain blue cast to the white shaving cream he always used.

He dressed in a lightweight dark gray Hopsack suit, a white shirt, and a maroon and blue paisley tie. He left his felt bedroom slippers on while he went downstairs and fixed himself coffee, toast, and two four-minute soft-boiled eggs. He read a paper called "Pathological Weeping" by Phyllis Greenacre in a 1945 issue of *The Psychoanalytic Quarterly* as he ate his breakfast. Then he went back upstairs to brush his teeth, put his wallet in his jacket pocket, and slip his feet into his black calfskins, propping them against the footstool as he laced them. He combed his hair and took a clean white handkerchief from the top drawer of the bureau. The bureau was an old blockfront, a Goddard; Margaret and he had found it at an auction in—

Neal slammed the drawer shut without allowing himself to finish the thought.

Officer Baird said, "Have you ever seen a pin like any of these?"

Except for the different Zodiac faces, they were the same

style. Neal pointed to the one with the virgin on its face.

"My wife has one like that. It's her Zodiac sign. Virgo."

"Do you know where she got it?"

"She never told me."

"It came from Harris Brothers. Shortly after your wife received it, she took it in for an adjustment. The clasp on the back didn't work properly. None of the clasps do. That's why Oscar Harris had planned to return the whole shipment to the manufacturer."

"What do you mean after my wife *received* it?"

"I'm getting to that, Doctor . . . The entire shipment was stolen from Harris Brothers. They reported it, but they really never expected to see the pins again. Oscar thought the thief would at least have the good sense to dispose of them out of town . . . Then your wife walked in wearing one of them. Oscar asked her where she got it. She told him a friend had given it to her and told her it was from Harris Brothers. Oscar asked her who the friend was, and Mrs. Dana was evasive. She said it was just a friend. Well, Oscar didn't want to embarrass her. He made the adjustment for her, and he reported it to me."

"Did you ask my wife about it?"

"I didn't have to," the policeman said. "The next day someone else came in with the same pin. Linda Chayka. She told Oscar who gave her the pin. It was Forrest Bissel. She goes out with him sometimes."

"I see," Neal said.

"*Do* you?"

"What do you mean?"

"This isn't easy for me, Dr. Dana. I've seen a few things— you can't help it in my job—things I'd just soon not have seen."

"Like what?" Neal asked, and then the policeman told him about coming across Margaret and Forrest in the Volkswagen, and about Minnie Nickerson's description of a "Titian-haired" prowler.

"Ordinarily, I don't pay a lot of attention to Minnie and her mother," Tom Baird said, "but I'd already seen Mrs. Dana and Forrest down by the river. I'm damn sorry I have to embarrass you like this, Dr. Dana."

"I know. I'm sorry it's necessary."

"We picked Forrest up last Friday. He was released in five hundred dollars bail until yesterday when there was supposed to be a hearing. Some relative in Spring Valley put up the bail money. So he claimed. I don't know if I believe that."

"What do you mean?"

"Perhaps Mrs. Dana got the bail money to him . . . He's skipped bail, Dr. Dana."

"I see."

"I know this isn't—"

Neal interrupted. "Just go ahead."

"This is what I think happened. They were planning to leave town together. She used your argument as a camouflage, so you'd think that was why she left. She went someplace nearby to wait until Bissel could get away. But Forrest was stalling her. We all know Forrest: he has a habit of stealing when he wants out of a situation. He wants to get caught. I figure he was trying to find a way out, back when he stole the pins. He was waiting to get caught. We picked him up, and I think Mrs. Dana got the bail money to him. Then I figure she talked him out of standing trial. Either way he's headed for jail; she probably convinced him to have a good time with her first. I know it doesn't make Mrs. Dana look very good, but I figure she must have gotten all mixed up in her thinking to be hanging around with him in the first place."

Neal lit a cigarette. He said, "Do you really think my wife would run off with Forrest Bissel?"

"I'm afraid I do, Dr. Dana. According to Linda Chayka, Mrs. Dana planned to take him on some sort of camping trip."

"Forrest told Linda Chayka about this?"

The policeman nodded. "Linda thought he was just a braggart, trying to impress her with this story of the older woman who was in love with him."

Neal winced involuntarily at the words "in love with him."

Tom Baird said, "But now she thinks that's what happened. I went to see her yesterday, looking for Forrest, and she told me about it. I didn't think it was that serious, Dr. Dana. That's why I didn't mention it on Saturday when you stopped by. I just didn't think her disappearance had anything to do with him."

"What did you think?" Neal asked, remembering the smile that had played on the policeman's lips when Neal had reported Margaret's absence to him.

"Oh, I suppose the thing with Forrest crossed my mind. But Forrest wasn't missing then. I didn't link the two together until I knew he'd skipped."

"And you actually think they're together?"

"Yes, Dr. Dana. There's no need for it to become public information. I suppose there'll be some talk. Linda Chayka will probably gossip, but then she's not a very credible gossip, is she? I doubt she knows the same people you do, either."

"Still—" Neal said.

"Yes, there'll be some talk. Most people won't believe it."

"No, they won't," said Neal. "And those who will, won't understand that Margaret deserves help now, not blame."

"Yes," Baird agreed. Then he said, "I don't think there's any help for Forrest. You did so much for him—and this is the way he repays you. He's a bad apple."

Impulsively, Neal decided to say, "The sister's not much better. She comes to the clinic now and then. You know the type—always worried that she's pregnant, and never certain which one made her that way." Neal forced a little laugh.

The policeman shuffled through some papers on his desk and didn't answer Neal. Neal had the sudden feeling that he was embarrassed, and then another idea came to his head: could there have been more behind the smile on Officer Baird's face that day than the knowledge of Margaret's affair with Forrest? Was it conceivable that the policeman had good reason to know that Margaret, too, had been the type Neal had just described? Perhaps on those few spontaneous visits to the Danas' he had hoped to find Margaret alone. Perhaps there had been many occasions when he had.

*May I ask you something,* Margaret had been in the habit of saying, and Neal had often suspected there was a patronizing flavor to the question, for Margaret usually had her own way. But how blind to her ways could he have been? How imperceptive a man was Dr. Neal Dana?

For the first time in his life he felt he knew nothing at all about himself . . . and as for Margaret . . .

But he could not accept such a concept of her for long. Hours later, as Penny Bissel sat across from him in his office, he totally rejected all thoughts of Margaret as a promiscuous woman.

Sick, yes.

And it had been his fault; it had come about because of his neglect of her. His vanity had been to blame for Margaret's involvement with Forrest, his insufferable fantasies of fame and sensuality.

While he listened to Penny, watching her face with that certain detachment which found new flaws in her features at every encounter, he determined to notify Doubleday that he was not prepared at this time to undertake the book.

". . . made up my mind that I'm going to have the baby whether you marry me or not, Neal," she was saying, "because I have to live with my conscience, and I've got enough on my conscience already. I've done enough!"

"What have you done?" he said. "You didn't hurt anyone. Someone got hurt in your presence, but you didn't do it."

"I know, but—"

"*Did* you?"

"Neal, I told you! I didn't touch her! I remember it like it happened this morning."

While she recalled it again in detail, Neal remembered

something that seemed so long ago, in such another time, that it became like an old man's memory of the boy he had been, viewed as though he were a stranger whose reasons for doing things and feeling them were no longer quite clear, and what had happened was unreal. Unreal—an afternoon when she had run toward him through the tall elephant grass, and the scent of sun in her hair when he caught her to him, and her fingers held on to his shirt, both of them laughing so hard until he told her solemnly, "I love you. Pen, I want you, because I love you."

"... believe me, Neal?" she asked.

"Yes."

She started to cry, and as he left his desk and went across to sit beside her on the leather couch he felt a prick of irritation at the fact her mascara was running again, as it had the last time he had been with her.

"You mustn't keep going over the same old ground," he told her, taking one of her hands in both of his.

"Then why did you say 'did you?'" she said. "Why did you say 'you didn't do it, *did* you?'"

"Honey," he said. "You weren't listening. I said, 'You know you didn't hurt her, *don't* you?'"

"I'm all mixed up, I guess."

"And no wonder," he said brushing his lips against her hair. "It's been a bad day for you."

"For you, too, darling."

"Don't worry about me. What we're concerned about is you, Pen."

"You don't have to marry me, Neal."

"That isn't why I want to marry you," he said, kissing her fingers, "because I *have* to."

"You want to marry me, Neal?" Her shoulders shook as she began to cry all the harder, and she threw her arms around him. He felt the dampness of her tears on his shirt with a twinge of revulsion.

"I want to marry you, Pen, of course I do."

"Oh, God, Neal! Oh, thank God, Neal! I thought I'd lost you."

"Shhh. Hush, honey . . . Now, of course I'm going to marry you. I have to figure everything out, so we do it just right, but of course I'm going to marry you."

"And you don't want me to have an abortion?"

"You said you wouldn't."

"I won't. But that's what you want, isn't it?"

"I want what you want," he said.

"I want to get married."

"Then that's what we'll do. But we'll have to keep it secret for a while. You'll have to go away to have the baby. We won't be able to live here."

"I know, I know," she kept murmuring.

"The only advantage to an abortion," he said, "is that it would make it so much easier for us to marry . . . You see, if I move away, if I suddenly acquire a wife and baby, I'll be giving them good reason to suspect that I had something to do with Margaret's disappearance."

"Neal," she said. "Can we stretch out on the couch for a few minutes? Just stretch out and put our arms around each other?"

"Oh, honey—"

"The door's locked. Just for a few minutes?"

"All right," he said.

As she fixed herself against him, he remembered something he had read once: the heaviest thing in the world is the body of someone you have ceased to love.

"Doesn't this feel good, darling?"

"Yes."

"We needed this, Neal. To be close. Even if we don't do anything, we need to have our bodies close. Like married people."

"Ummm hmmm."

"I felt funny lying to the doctor about being married. I don't think he believed me."

"You'll never have to see him again."

"But I felt funny lying. He's a doctor, you know? An M.D. I hate to lie to a real doctor."

"How about lying to a Ph.D.? Do you hate to do that, too?" He smiled.

She clung hard to him, with a strength that belied her size. Once, years ago when Margaret and he had owned several cats, Neal had had to drown the runt in one of their litters. It had amazed him how hard the little animal had died, how much power it had summoned forth in the effort to survive.

"I didn't really lie to you, Neal," Penny answered his question. "I just didn't tell you *why* Daddy went to Spring Valley that Friday."

"That's lying by omission, sweetheart," he said softly.

"I didn't want to tell you he'd gone over there to get bail for Forrest. I didn't want you to know Forrest was in trouble again."

"But why? I know your brother pretty well by now."

"I thought it would reflect on me, and if we're going to have a baby, I don't want you thinking things like what kind of relatives he'll have on my side."

A dart of hope shot through Neal at the "if." He brought his hand down to her breasts, caressing them lightly. "Pen? Did you hear what I said about the advantage to an abortion?"

"You haven't done that in a long time, Neal. Like, I thought you forgot all about them, darling."

"I didn't, though, not for a moment . . . Pen, did you hear what I said?"

"Uh huh."

"And there's your father to consider, how we'll handle him, what we'll tell him. Do you see how complicated it is?"

"You can figure it out, Neal. I know you can."

"But we have to look at all the angles, sweetheart," he said.

"Uh huh."

"Before it's too late for you to have an abortion."

"You can think what you want about Forrest," she said, "but that's one thing he's dead set against. He says it's murder."

"*Forrest?*" He gave a derisive chuckle.

"Yes, Forrest . . . Neal, please don't hate him."

"I don't hate him. I pity him."

"You're not mad because of what the police think about your wife and him?"

"I told you, Penny, they're wrong. And *you* know they're wrong. Because you know Margaret's whereabouts, don't you?"

"But maybe Forrest *was* seeing her!"

"You saw Margaret," said Neal. "Do you think a woman like Margaret would have anything to do with your brother?"

"You shouldn't say things like that, Neal." She took his hands away from her breasts. "I don't like it."

"Well, do you?" he said. He placed his hands back where they were, smiling down at her. "You saw her," he said.

"He's still my brother." She tried to jerk away from his touch. He held her fast.

"And Margaret was my wife."

"A lot of people like Forrest."

"Ask your aunt in Spring Valley what she thinks of him, now that she's out five hundred dollars bail money."

"She's crazy about Forrest. He gave her one of those astrology pins, too."

Neal said, "But he let her five hundred dollars go down the drain, didn't he?"

"It's not like him. I don't know why he did. He gave her one of those pins. Her and I are the same sign."

"*She* and I."

"She and I. We're both Pisces like Elizabeth Taylor."

"*Really?*" Neal said with exaggerated enthusiasm.

"Let me up, Neal."

"We need this, Pen," he said. "Even if we don't do anything. Even if we do," he said, pushing his hand up under her sweater.

"Don't act so superior then, Neal. Your own wife was interested in astrology. She could have said the exact same thing I just said."

"You think that?"

"Yes . . . Neal, don't. You're too rough with me there."

"That Margaret would bother to link herself with some movie actress. You think that?"

"Neal, don't treat me this way. I've just been to the doctor."

"You don't know anything about Margaret, do you, except that she's in a hole in the woods."

"*Neal!*"

"Do you? Do you know anything about her?"

"No," she said in a frightened voice. "What's the matter with you, Neal?"

"So don't talk about Margaret, do you hear?"

"You're hurting me, Neal. Those are new stockings."

"Or Margaret and Forrest, do you hear?"

And he remembered the runt cat again as she worked her arms free from his weight and punched his chest with her fists. "Don't *you* talk about Forrest the way you do, either," she said angrily. "Because a lot of stuff isn't our fault!" She spit out the words. "We had bad childhoods, and you of all people ought to know that!"

With one hand he pinned her arms around her back.

"That's why I'd never do anything to hurt *my* baby!" she said.

There was black mascara smudged down her cheeks, as there had been last Friday when he had sat beside her in the kitchen and believed that he could never touch her again.

"What are you doing, Neal? Why are you doing it this way?"

And he was fascinated by the fight in her, the look in her eyes, as though she feared for her life, and he rode hard on this, until ultimately she moved in rhythm with him at the moment he came; then the illusion went.

CHAPTER 19

The night before when Archie had called his service, there was a message that Ken Granger from CBS wanted to see him. Since Archie was going into New York today anyway, he called Ken's secretary and set up an eleven-thirty appointment. He had spoken with the producer on Monday and Ken had told Archie that an angry Mrs. Muckermann had been waiting in his office when he arrived that morning, and that the astrology special was being shelved.

Archie clung to a feather of hope that Ken might have something else in mind. Archie badly needed work. He was outlining the thing on symbiotic relations to give his agent, and he had an afternoon appointment with George Walsh at *Cosmopolitan* to discuss article ideas, but no project lined up yet that wasn't speculative. CBS still had to pay him another twenty-five hundred despite the fact the show wasn't going on, but he had counted on considerably more that that, and the first-of-the-month bills, which were beginning to roll in, showed it. His nerves were on edge as a result, and Dru was reacting to his moodiness, half-convinced that all the Mrs. Muckermann propaganda about his being badly aspected was

161

true. They had been able to kid about it before, but more and more it started out light and ended up heavy . . . More and more everything between them did.

Archie's Triumph was finally ready at the garage in Nyack, and he picked it up at nine that morning, put the top down, and plugged along in commuter traffic, arriving in New York at ten-twenty. He left the car at the Hippodrome on 44th Street, and went across to the Algonquin to phone Liddy.

When he was down, Liddy always had a soothing effect on him. She had known him way back in the days when he had been happy to receive a hundred dollars from *Reader's Digest* for a filler, and when he could paper their apartment walls with his rejection slips. Dru took his free-lance career for granted, but Liddy had lived through the birth pangs and ex- perienced the oscillations—then, being no fool, Liddy had reacted by becoming a fortune-hunter. Like a father who had raised his child in the slums, Archie didn't blame her for "aspiring," for wanting to be free of the endless, inevitable worry over money. In fact, Archie no longer blamed Liddy for anything, nor looked for anything from her but a laugh, amity, and the sharing of a lot of old memories. So he told himself. And hadn't it been confirmed by their last meeting? No strings, any more, and no regrets: just a good feeling . . . Why not flowers for his birthday?

"Thanks for the flowers," he said when she answered.

"Did I have the date right?"

"You were early. What's all the noise in the background?"

"I'm moving out. My things are going in storage."

"You just moved in."

"A woman's privilege, Archie. I've got so much to tell you."

"Do you want to have lunch? I'm in town."

"I'd love it! I've got wonderful news. I'll tell you at lunch. I hope you'll think it's wonderful."

He said, "Just don't bubble too much when you tell me. My news is all low tide . . . I've got an appointment on the West

Side at CBS, so how about the Italian Pavilion around quarter to one?"

"I can't wait that long to tell you this much," she said. "Either we're finally legally divorced, or I'm a bigamist."

"Congratulations!" he barked out too heartily. "Wonderful!"

"I'm so happy, Archie!"

"You're bubbling, Liddy," he warned her, still accommodating the punch of shock inside him.

"And *I'm* taking *you* to lunch," she said.

"Is he rich? Silly question."

"As a matter of fact, he isn't."

"I thought I had you trained."

"This time I'm really in love, Archie. I want you to remember that when you meet him."

"Why? Did you marry Rap Brown? Spiro Agnew? J. Edgar Hoover? Mayor Daley?"

"Just remember," Liddy said. "I love him, Archie."

It was unlikely that he would forget that.

Ken Granger was talking on the telephone when Archie arrived. He was listening more than he was talking, and he waved Archie to a seat and passed him a sheet of paper, motioning for him to look it over.

It was a memo from a CBS researcher re: ONE WORD DESCRIPTIONS OF ZODIAC TYPES.

| | |
|---|---|
| ARIES | dynamic |
| TAURUS | stable |
| GEMINI | vascillating |
| CANCER | protective |
| LEO | dominating |
| VIRGO | efficient |
| LIBRA | compromising |
| SCORPIO | passionate |

SAGITTARIUS ........................................... adventuresome

CAPRICORN ............................................... scheming

AQUARIUS .................................................. humanitarian

PISCES ............................................................... mystic

When Ken finally hung up, he said, "That was Herself giving me the business."

"Mrs. Muckermann?"

Ken nodded. "She says we're going to be slapped with a lawsuit if we do the show without her."

"Is it on again?"

"I think so, Archie. But not with her. The woman's insane."

"*Tell* me," Archie said.

"She told me you're going to do something violent, if you haven't already done it, and I'm the way I am because I was born with the Sun in Leo, same as Mussolini, Huey Long and Napoleon . . . all of whom, she added, came to a bad end."

Archie laughed and said, "I wondered what was wrong with you, Ken. So you're a Leo. She left out Cesare Borgia and Fidel Castro."

"She's colorful," said Ken, "and she'd come across as a real character, but I didn't realize she was all the way around the bend. If we used her, it'd be like we were giving her an endorsement."

"Who are you going to get?"

"No one, for that very reason. We can't give anyone an endorsement. I see that now." He reached for a cigarette, saying: "Still interested in writing it, or have you had it?"

"Still interested."

He lit the cigarette. "Good . . . I want to send that memo down to publicity. Do you agree with it? We want to work out some teasers—nothing profound. Simple stuff like that."

"It looks reasonable," Archie said. Then he chuckled.

"What's funny?"

"Libra. Compromising. Mrs. Muckermann's a Libra."

"Okay, cross it out and substitute 'maniacal.'"

"I wouldn't quarrel with any of it," Archie said. "It's about as close as you can come with one word."

Ken said, "We'll run one teaser with the one-word description, and then another one with a famous person after each sign. Research is going to work on that next."

"I can pencil them in right away, if you want."

"Fine. Call them out. I don't want any Mussolinis or Cesare Borgias."

"Let's see," said Archie, "Aries, Charlie Chaplin."

"Hold it! Nobody controversial."

"Charlie Chaplin?"

"Give me another."

"How's Marlon Brando?"

"Okay."

"Taurus, Harry Truman . . . Gemini, John Kennedy."

"Kennedy's out," said Ken. "It'll just call up the assassination. We don't want any bad omens."

"All right, Gemini: the Duchess of Windsor."

"Good . . . Can you come up with a Negro now?"

"I can't think of one who's Cancer," Archie said. "I'll keep it in mind. For Cancer, how about Nelson Rockefeller?"

"Okay," Ken said. "But let's not have all WASPs."

"Bernard Baruch for Leo."

"Right."

"Virgo, Leonard Bernstein."

"We've got a Jew."

"How's Grandma Moses then?"

"That's it."

"Libra . . . Mahatma Gandhi?"

"Someone younger, Archie; you just threw in Grandma Moses."

"Brigitte Bardot?"

"She'll do . . . What's next?"

"Scorpio; how about Katharine Hepburn?"

"I don't think of her as passionate," said Ken.

"Do you think of Brigitte Bardot as compromising?"

Ken smiled. "I can see her meeting someone halfway."

"All right. Scorpio, Mata Hari."

"Great."

"Sagittarius, Frank Sinatra."

Ken nodded.

"Capricorn, Aristotle Onassis."

Ken said, "What's her sign?"

"Jackie? She's a Leo. Capricorns and Leos aren't good together, according to Mrs. Muckermann. Leo's supposedly too strong and quick for Capricorn."

"I'll bet on him anyway," Ken said. "Aquarius is next."

"Here's your Negro, Ken: Marian Anderson."

"We've got a lot of women, haven't we?"

"Where's your biggest appeal going to be?"

"Yes. The ladies, I suppose."

"Pisces, Jackie Gleason."

"A mystic? *Gleason?*"

"How's Albert Einstein?"

"Fine," said Ken. He asked his secretary to run the memo down to Publicity; then he tipped back in his swivel chair, stuck his feet up on the desk, and asked Archie how things had worked out with his "astro-twin."

"It's not promising," said Archie. "Oh, there *are* similarities. We have to reach for them, though. We could do it. I could write it up dramatically. But—"

Granger leaned forward to pull another memo off his desk top.

"Donald Chapman and Donald Brazill were born at the same time exactly, in neighboring California towns," he read. "Five days after their twenty-third birthday, they met on U.S. 101, by crashing head-on. It was their first meeting. They both died in the wreck. It was discovered later that they did the same kind of work, lived in the same locality, and had almost identical lives." He looked across at Archie. "You want to hear more?"

"No. That's from Joseph Goodavage's book."

"You know it?"

"Yes. Look, Ken, there's no doubt the thing has happpened to people; it's all been documented."

"This Goodavage claims that in one hundred percent of the cases investigated, there was a parallelism."

"There's not much of one between my 'astro-twin' and me. At least not so far, that *I* can see."

"Mrs. Muckermann said she could see it."

"Oh, there's something there, all right, if you strain."

"Listen to this," said Ken. "Millie Burton and Robert Harris. Both born in 1949, same hour, a minute apart, Bayshore, Long Island. Millie lost a brother in Vietnam. So did Robert. Millie owns a Dachshund named Pork. Robert owns one named Piggy. Millie wants to be a lawyer. Robert's in pre-law at N.Y.U. Millie is a boating enthusiast. Robert owns a sailboat. They've never met, but both now live in New York in the Chelsea area." He put the memo back on the desk. "What do you think of it?"

"Millie Burton? Why is the name familiar?"

"She works in our legal department. She was one of the names we used on our ads."

"And Robert answered?"

"His mother did . . . How's it sound? Millie got all the information over the phone, but it sounds pretty interesting already."

"A hell of a lot more interesting than what I've come up with," said Archie.

"Robert's spending his vacation with his mother in Bay Shore. You want to run out there tomorrow and have a look at him?"

"Right. Will Millie come along?"

"I think she should."

They were still discussing ideas for the special at twelve-fifteen, and Ken suggested sending out for Chinese food from Pearl's. Archie called Liddy to cancel the lunch date. He said he'd meet her for a drink around fourish; she agreed to check the time and place with his service since she was off to Saks and Best's and Bonwit's.

By the time Archie connected with her, at the Algonquin near five, he was bubbling, too. Ken had come up with a lot of good, workable ideas, and Archie had talked George Walsh into an article about women who found success by teaming with men other than their husbands: Imogene Coca, Elaine May, Jeanette MacDonald, and others.

Liddy looked radiant in a new Pucci she had bought at Saks. They found a corner in the small, dark bar near the entrance and ordered Rob Roys.

Archie lit her Gauloise.

"You're first," Liddy said. "Why are you at low tide?"

He started explaining that he wasn't any more, but when he had finished telling her the good news about the special and the article for *Cosmo,* he found himself describing all the petty bickering which was persisting between Dru and himself, and then all the business about Neal and life thus far in the country.

Liddy put her hand over his and said, "I won't let you worry this way, Archie," and he remembered all the times in the past when just her saying that had made him feel better. He felt deliciously protected in the aromatic cocoon of Gauloise smoke intermingled with the fragrance of Celui, all so familiar, and he forgot to call Dru and tell her that he had to go to Bay Shore next day and he wouldn't be home that night.

When he finally did think of it, Liddy was just about to tell him about her new husband. It was near seven—past the dinner hour—and he had to spring up in the middle of what she was saying and run out to the phone booth by the newsstand.

He got as far as, "I won't be home tonight," when Dru interrupted and told him that that was just fine with her and hung up.

He was so enraged by her refusal to allow him to explain that he almost didn't recognize his own father when he collided with him near a divan in the lobby.

Frank Gamble grinned and said, "Well, where's my blushing bride, son?"

CHAPTER 20

"Sweetie, I don't want to upset you, but there are responsibilities one simply has to undertake. A doctor has to warn and advise, and steel himself against the consequences, and so does a lawyer."

"Mrs. Muckermann," said Dru, pushing Tiffany away from her chicken sandwich, "you're not a doctor, you're not a lawyer."

"But I have a profession which necessitates both diagnosis and counsel," said Mrs. Muckermann. " 'Knowledge,' as John Milton once wrote, 'by favour sent, Down from the empyrean to forewarn, Us timely.' Druscilla, dear, this is a critical time in Archie's chart. Venus is squaring Saturn, and with all the other bad aspects, the violence brewing and the building of evil forces, I can't imagine that the country is very peaceful for you, that you're happy out there."

Dru slapped the Siamese on the behind finally. The cat hissed at her and fled under the table. Dru leaned back on the couch, nestling the telephone between her neck and her shoulder, as she munched on her chicken sandwich. She said, "I'm sorry it wasn't more peaceful last Saturday, Mrs. Muckermann. We'd had a lot of champagne, and we were being silly; we didn't mean to hurt your feelings."

"You didn't hurt my feelings, Archie hurt them. And Archie can't help himself. When Venus squares Saturn, there's no attempt to spare *anyone's* feelings. I'm sure you've been on the receiving end of his fiery little impulses to be cruel, too."

Dru swallowed the bite of the sandwich and took a swig of Fresca. "Well, for Pete's sake, tell us what to do about it, then," she said. "A doctor would, a lawyer would."

"And I would, too," said Mrs. Muckermann, "normally. But Archie won't cooperate."

"Then tell me. I'll go to work on him."

"He should use his Jupiter, Druscilla. Jupiter can save him."

"Save him from what?"

"Paranoia, hypocrisy, and an icy detachment at intervals which Venus squaring Saturn invariably calls forth. Fury—Saturn again, and a conscienceless attitude brought about by our old friend Mercury."

Dru said, "Aren't we asking a lot of Jupiter?"

"Jupiter can handle a lot. Anyone with Pisces to rule can handle a lot, and Jupiter rules both Pisces and Sagittarius, remember."

"Mrs. Muckermann," Dru said tiredly, "can you just tell me, please, some practical suggestions? I don't understand it when you're philosophizing. How does Archie get Jupiter to work for him?"

"Jupiter operates in the liver and intestines, some say the arms, too . . . but my advice is for Archie to go easy with alcohol. Too much of it always insults the liver and intestines."

And Anna Muckermann, last Saturday night, Dru thought to herself.

"What else?"

"Thursday's Jupiter's day—that's why I called today. This could be a crucial day, sweetie. Jove, Jeudi, Thor's day, Thursday—regardless of the language, it's Jupiter's day. There'll be expansion today. That's Jupiter's keyword. Expansion. It could be good, but if one isn't wary, sweetie, it could be bad. It could lead to gambling, dissipation, extravagance, risk-taking. Do you see?"

"I'll pass the word along."

"Negatively, Jupiter will exaggerate difficulties, and then can't do the job at hand, but positively—"

"Yes, yes? Did I hear you say the word 'positively'?" said Dru.

"Positively," said Mrs. Muckermann with a sudden lilt to her tone, "Jupiter will expand and multiply."

Dru groaned inwardly. Full circle again to Lane Bryant.

In the daytime, none of it bothered her as much. At night, all of it did, for there was something eerie about nighttime in the country after being so long in the city. The night no longer belonged to buses which snorted down Third Avenue, and college boys who came trooping out of Joe King's loaded on beer and lustily singing "Banging Away on Lulu"; there were no late-late show sounds from the neighbors next door, no police or ambulance sirens . . . nothing but katy-did and katy-didn't, crickets squeaking and frogs chortling, an occasional foghorn from the river, and overhead all the stars. The goddamn stars . . . Dru could remember back to her salad days when the only bad thing that ever came to mind when she glanced up at the stars was the idea of one falling . . . someone dying. Now they seemed as malefic as they might be had China or Russia managed to man them all with nuclear missiles.

Tiffany was back, winding in and out of Dru's legs, and she gave in and took the chicken out of the other half of the sandwich, feeding it to the cat while she purred and let her crossed eyes droop half-closed in ecstasy.

"So lay off the robins now," Dru told her. "Live and let live, Tiffany."

Archie had left a list of books he wanted her to borrow from the Nyack library, and after Dru finished another chapter of *More Work for the Undertaker* by Margaret Allingham, she slipped on a dress, pushed Tiffany out of the Cages' Buick, and headed toward town.

She parked up near the Pickwick Book Store where she killed half an hour deciding whether to buy *David Smith by David Smith* or face the fact Archie and she couldn't afford twenty-two ninety-five for a book, despite the fact he was their favorite sculptor; she settled ultimately for a paperback Gothic by Mary Stewart.

Then to the five-and-ten to look for a button to match the one Archie had lost from his tan cardigan, and next door to to the Sweete Shoppe for a hot chocolate sundae with peanuts on top.

"*'Madam Will You Talk?'*"

"What?" She turned around and found Neal Dana reading aloud the title of her Mary Stewart.

"The ice cream looks good," he said. "May I join you?"

"Sure. Welcome to your first meeting of the We're Fat And We Like It That Way club."

He laughed and swung his long leg over the counter stool. "I never get any ice cream at home. Margaret's a member of We're *Not* Fat and We'll Keep It That Way." He smiled down at Dru. "Fat's better. It's like what someone said about money. I've been poor and I've been rich, and rich is better."

"*You* don't have to count calories."

"You don't, either," he said, and Dru wished he hadn't happened along because it reminded her she wasn't wearing a girdle, and she had to sit with her stomach sucked in now.

She said, "Neal, I want to tell you again how sorry Archie and I are about what happened to poor Sinister."

"It wasn't anyone's fault," he said. "I don't know how Tiffany opened the cage."

"Oh, I do. She could open the Chase Manhattan vault if

she thought there was a bird inside. Archie put a bell on her collar Monday morning, and Monday afternoon we looked out to see her heading across the lawn in her best hunter's crouch, three-legged, holding the bell with her right front paw."

Neal laughed again, ordered a butterscotch sundae, and lit a True. "Is Archie home pounding the typewriter?"

"He had to go into New York to see an editor . . . Hey, Neal, don't you see the Doubleday people this week?"

"That's all off."

"*What?*"

"I'm not ready anyway."

"Did they call it off?"

He gave her a noncommittal shrug. "I never should have gotten involved in the thing. That would be fun for Margaret, wouldn't it? I'd come home every night and lock myself in my study."

"I don't *believe* this!" said Dru. "Archie loses his show on Monday, and now you've lost your book!"

"The 'astro-twins' lose again."

"Are you *ready* for this?" Dru said.

"I didn't exactly lose it," said Neal.

Dru didn't believe him.

"I wasn't thinking of Margaret," he said.

Dru decided the subject embarrassed him, and in a hurry to steer away from it she went back to Sinister.

"Archie and I would like to get Margaret a new bird."

"No. She isn't really a bird-lover. It was just Sinister."

"I'm sorry."

"I know."

"I was so upset I tried to call you the minute I found him. You didn't answer."

He said, "I didn't sleep. We had so much coffee. I knew Tiffany'd killed him when I saw her take him into the woods."

He shrugged. "I felt like company so I went down to Sbordone's for a beer."

"You did?" Archie hadn't said anything about Neal showing up at Sbordone's. "What time, Neal?"

"I don't know exactly. Right after Tiffany headed for the woods."

"It was four o'clock when she brought Sinister home."

"Oh, she got him *long* before that. But it's quite a distance from our house to the Cages'. She probably took her time, too. You know how cats play with birds."

"What was it, around three?"

"Around midnight. I left shortly after for Sbordone's."

"Oh."

"I stayed until closing. Some old movie was on the TV in the bar."

"And you had company?"

"Hmmm?" He frowned at her.

"You said you felt like company, so you went to Sbordone's."

"Yeah. There were a few of the regulars."

But not Archie, that was obvious.

Then where was Archie for those three or four hours?

At that time of night, when there was almost no traffic, it was possible to reach New York in thirty minutes.

Dru didn't feel like finishing the rest of her sundae.

Neal said, "Why all the concern?"

"Oh, nothing . . . A little marital spat that'll probably end up in a court of law," she said ironically.

"Did Archie go to Sbordone's Saturday night, too? There were some people drinking in the other room."

"Archie drinks at a bar."

"Maybe we just missed each other."

"I don't know."

"You don't have to worry about Archie."

"Famous last words."

"Do you?"

"I don't know what I have to worry about any more, or who. It's gotten so I even worry about Saturn, and Venus squaring Saturn, and never rely on Gemini, and all the rest of Mrs. Muckermann's reassuring wisdom."

Neal said, "Dru?"

"What?"

"This is going to sound paranoiac, but I was thinking something this morning . . . Is there any possibility, *remote* possibility, that Archie and Margaret might have met somewhere?"

"*Huh?*"

"I just thought maybe there was a slight possibility they had."

"No, Neal."

"They could have."

"*No*, Neal."

"Why are you so adamant about it? They could have."

"They didn't. *That* I know. I kid you not."

"I wasn't trying to make anything out of it."

"Neither Archie nor I have ever met Margaret. I spoke to her on the phone. That's it."

He said, "You see, I've been so self-absorbed. So caught up in my own sails. Margaret was left to . . ." His voice trailed off and he didn't finish. The waitress placed the butterscotch sundae in front of him.

"You'd both like Margaret," he said after he had a spoonful of the ice cream. "She's a wonderful person."

"I'm sure she is, Neal. But believe me, Archie never even heard of her before I told him about her letter."

"Maybe you're protesting too much."

"I'm protesting a lot, because I know that the mind plays funny tricks when you're upset."

"I guess so."

"I've had nights when I've decided Archie was playing around with every woman who lives on our floor and offering to take the garbage down to the incinerator just so he could pinch them good night."

Neal tried to laugh. "Margaret isn't the type who plays around," he said.

Dru didn't say anything; what do you say to that?

Neal said, "The mind does play tricks, you're right . . . No, Margaret is a woman with real integrity."

Dru looked away from him and rolled her eyes back in her head.

"She cares about things. The voting age, and learning Italian, and . . ." Again he didn't finish.

Then he finally said, "And she loves good music."

Dru borrowed one of his cigarettes and smoked it while she listened to him eulogize Margaret Dana. She only half-heard the eulogy; her thoughts were still back at Sbordone's . . . or New York—she was no longer certain about anything.

Neal had a three-thirty appointment with the welfare bureau concerning a patient at Rock-Or whose family needed assistance, and he walked Dru down to the library on his way.

The card catalogue showed that the library had the books Archie wanted on Burgess and Maclean, Laurel and Hardy, and Lewis and Clark; Dru copied the numbers on a piece of note paper and headed for the open stacks. She was vaguely aware of a woman sharing the stacks with her, but as she searched for 707.30, Dru was preoccupied by the first really guilty feelings she had suffered since she had talked Archie into keeping the letters and the diary belonging to Margaret Dana. Whatever she wasn't able to figure out about the mystery attached to Neal's wife—Archie seeing her the other night, all of it—she was able to perceive that Neal obviously didn't know the facts and was tortured by conflicting judgments of her: she was a saint he was unworthy of; she was an indiscriminate trollop who had dallied with everyone imaginable, including Archie . . . *Paranoia, which Venus squaring Saturn invariably calls forth;* Neal himself had used the word "paranoiac."

Dru found two of the books she was looking for; the third

was missing. She carried her books to a table near the newspaper racks and found a copy of yesterday's New York *Post*. In New York she read the *Post* faithfully every day, but out here it was hard to find a newsstand that carried it. She missed Max Lerner and Drew Pearson; she had lost track of Mary Worth's new "case" and Abby's latest advice to "Taken Advantage Of" and "Wife Of An Alcoholic."

She settled down to enjoy the *Post* as though she were pausing for a cup of coffee with an old friend. She read Harriet Van Horne, glanced at Nancy and Dennis the Menace, and then her eye caught Carroll Righter's column, *In the Stars*. The predictions always pertained to the following day; she looked for hers for Thursday, today, under "Moon Children," which some astrologers now chose in preference to the dread word "Cancer."

> You have some responsibility
> that you want to renege on, but
> this would lead to trouble. Why
> don't you help that person who
> is in trouble?

Both sentences ended with the word "trouble."
Right, folks?
She sighed and naturally thought of a way this little message could pertain to her. It was her responsibility to return the letters and the diary; it was up to her to help Neal. Even if the truth hurt, it probably wouldn't hurt as badly as the exaggerations Neal's anxieties were conjuring up.

But she was the chicken's chicken, friends; the only way she could imagine herself carrying it off was to deposit Tuto's mewings and Margaret Dana's musings on Neal's porch by dark of night, the way bastards are given over to orphanages.

She'd have to sneak up the hill on foot, and then undoubtedly suffer herself being sacrificed to Kendal as she came back down: Fate would surely penalize her in some way like that.

What were Gemini's chances for Thursday?

> You have a wild desire to make
> some hasty changes. Curb these
> impulses. They could later
> boomerang.

While she thought that one over, she glanced out the window toward the parking lot at the rear of the library. At first her mind did not register the significance of what her eyes watched: a woman getting into a car, the same woman she had noticed so fleetingly back in the stacks. She recognized the paisley-collared kelly green suit, all that she had really noticed about the woman. Then she recognized something else: the black Ford Falcon with the gold penny on the door. The car passed out of view before she could get a good look at Margaret Dana.

For a moment Dru simply sat there damning her luck. Then she remembered the section in the stacks where she had come upon the woman; she remembered that Margaret Dana had not moved from that section. Curious to know what she could have come to the library to look for, Dru went back to the stacks. All of the books along the shelf where Margaret Dana had been standing were in neat order, except four or five near the end. One was tipped forward, and Dru reached for it.

Its title was *The Pregnant Woman.*

Next to it was a Dr. Spock; beside that was *Expectant Motherhood.*

Dru didn't wait to take off her coat when she reached the Cages'. It was four-thirty; Archie usually checked with the answering service three or four times a day when he was out. If she could catch him before he started back to the country, she was going to suggest (insist?) that she drive in to meet him, that they spend the night at the apartment. On the drive from Nyack, she had started putting together the pieces:

Margaret Dana was expecting Tuto's child, that much was obvious. And Archie hadn't seen a mirage last Saturday night; Margaret Dana *was* still very much in the vicinity. Neal couldn't know it—everything about his actions said as much— yet she didn't seem to be making any secret of her where- abouts. She could easily have run into Neal as he was walking Dru to the library . . . Yet, Neal had said that it was unusual for him to be away from the clinic in the afternoon; Mar- garet Dana wouldn't have anticipated an encounter with him at that time of day in downtown Nyack. Anyone else, though; friends, the police—she certainly wasn't trying to hide.

The pieces didn't fit together. The more Dru tried to force them into a logical pattern, the more they refused any attempt at organization.

The thing that *was* beginning to crystallize was the thing that prompted Dru to call Archie and tell him she wanted a night back in their own place. For whatever else was askew, unfamiliar, mysterious, illogical—Mrs. Muckermann's presenti- ments were beginning to seem like the only sure thing. And as Dru dialed New York, a new thought occurred to her: what if it wasn't Tuto's baby at all, but Neal's? Mars, Neptune and Leo were in Neal's House of Offspring, right? What if Mar- garet Dana had just discovered she was pregnant as she was about to run off with Tuto? And what if she knew that it was Neal's baby? Weren't the later letters filled with references to broken dates, as though they weren't seeing each other very much at all? If she were newly pregnant, wouldn't it be Neal's child?

As soon as she gave the service a message for Archie to call, Dru intended to look through the letters and diary again, paying closer attention to the dates. But first she would try to reach Archie. She needed a night in town; they both did. Maybe see something wild off-off Broadway which would take the edge off this witches' cauldron out here; maybe drop in at La Mama, hopefully happen on a Megan Terry fantasy, whip down to Chinatown after for bean curd and wor shew duck.

"The Gambles' residence."

"Has Mr. Gamble checked in yet?"

"Yes, ma'am. He left a message for you. Just a minute."

Then before Dru could say anything to that, the Answer-phone girl returned on the line with this to say: "Miss Deny-ven? He'll meet you at the Algonquin at five."

"You'd better save that message for Miss Denyven," said Dru, and she dropped the phone back into its cradle.

By the time Archie called to say he was spending the night in New York, she had composed herself. Fearful of losing that composure, she kept it short and not very sweet.

Then she went back to finish the letter she had decided to write Neal Dana. It was a complete confession. She absolved Archie since he wasn't there to okay it.

She intended to drive up the hill and present it to Neal, along with the *billets-doux* and the diary.

She knew this much: she had played God long enough. And the thing about God was, He was dead, anyway; someone else was working the strings now: Jupiter, Saturn, Mercury, maybe the devil himself in drag as Mrs. Muckermann.

But Dru had had the subterfuge, the hypocrisy, and the in-trigue up to here! Undoubtedly, Fate was repaying her in kind for what she had done to Neal.

The phone rang a few times and Dru let it ring.

What was left to say to Archie?

So long, Oolong.

After she picked at a dinner of scrambled eggs and cottage cheese, she drove down River Road in the damp night, deter-mined to get it over with. Would she sit there while Neal read the words she couldn't have found the presence of mind to say, or would she simply hand him everything and leave im-mediately?

The coward in her told her to do the latter, then observed the shroud of fog hovering ominously around the Buick and turned the car around, heading back to the Cages'.

CHAPTER 21

Dear Neal,

Archie doesn't know any of this, so if you're going to hate someone, focus entirely on me.

These letters and the diary were in the Pan Am bag Margaret left in the Volkswagen.

I read them because that's the kind of unprincipled busybody I am. I didn't put them back in the bag, because I didn't feel you would have found them at all if we hadn't called your attention to the bag. I thought Margaret would come back and maybe you'd never have to know about it . . . Selfishly I thought that if the Gambles were the instrument to your finding out, you might not consent to the special . . . At the time, the special seemed to be the most important thing for Archie and me.

Everything will speak for itself, Neal, but as long as I'm telling you all this, let me add more. The night we came to your house for the first time, I noticed a car in the drive. I don't know whose car it is—perhaps you do. I wouldn't have paid any attention to it, except for the penny on the door. That struck me as a feminine touch, though I can see now that a boy might stick something like that on a car door, too. I saw the car again this afternoon at the library. If it is that Tuto's car, if it could be that Margaret drives it sometimes, then I saw Margaret. I don't know the significance of any of this, and

I'm too confused by my own life to think clearly—which is why I have to write this instead of saying it—but if it was Margaret I saw today, she was looking through some books on pregnancy. I didn't get a good look at her, but I'm certain about the books she was examining.

Maybe it'll shed some light on things for you—I hope so. I wouldn't blame you if you wanted nothing more to do with me, but I couldn't be more sorry, Neal—please believe that.

Dru.

CHAPTER 22

As though he were taking to dinner two small children who could not read, Frank Gamble recited aloud to Archie and Liddy the three dinner entrees on the menu at the Gramercy Park Hotel.

"Poached Filet of Lemon Sole, Bonne Femme; Whole Boneless Cornish Game Hen; and Prime Ribs of Blue Ribbon Beef. They all sound good to me!"

Archie had known they would all sound good to his father. Years of dissipation had left its mark on Frank Gamble's stomach. Whenever he was confronted with anything other than bland food, he began a lengthy, vivid recital of his ailments. Archie wasn't up to it tonight, which was the reason he had suggested the hotel.

It was just a few blocks from Archie's apartment, too. He could make a fast getaway after dinner, while Liddy and his father whiled away the few hours which would be left before they were due to catch an eleven-thirty flight to San Juan.

"This din-din won't be hard on the old tum-tum," said Frank Gamble, "and I thank you, son, for being thoughtful enough to choose this place."

Archie didn't dare look Liddy in the eye, for fear he would

see registered there his own feeling of embarrassment for her. He could not believe it had been anything but a last desperate decision which had motivated her to marry Frank Gamble, and he hated himself for failing to perceive her despair, for letting it come to this.

But then Liddy touched the sleeve of his jacket, and sought his eyes with her own, and hers were shining. She said, "You are a doll, Archie! I was sure we were in for garlic and snails and rodents' tails in some smart East Side bistro. Then I'd have to spoon Maalox down Daddy all the way to San Juan."

"You used to love French food," Archie said. "I can remember when you used to look down your nose at a good Christ Cella steak and long for frogs' legs over at some dump on the West Side."

"I didn't have Daddy to worry over then," she said.

Archie sighed. "Order the roast beef for me, please. I'm going to try to call Dru back again." He stood up. "And order me a double Dewar's, too."

When there was no answer, Archie slammed down the receiver angrily and checked the time again. It was a quarter to nine. One of Dru's favorite tricks was not to answer the phone when she was angry and aware that he was trying to reach her. He was just as angry at her for hanging up on him when he had called from the Algonquin; he was disinclined to persist in calling her back, but he had to let her know he was staying over because of the trip to Bay Shore tomorrow.

He damned her stubbornness and took it out on the door of the phone booth as he emerged, slamming it back with his elbow. Heads turned in the lobby, eyes stared . . . among them the enormous bluebird eyes of Anna Muckermann.

She was standing just to the right of the newsstand with another thin little woman clutching a Yorkie under her arm.

Archie had to pass them on his way back to the dining room. As he approached, Mrs. Muckermann said, "A hot temper leaps, ah?"

"I beg your pardon?"

She said, "I said, a hot temper leaps. A very famous Taurus once wrote, 'The brain may devise laws for the blood, but a hot temper leaps o'er a cold decree.'"

Her companion remarked softly, "William Shakespeare," and shifted the shivering Yorkie to her other arm.

Mrs. Muckermann said, "Yes. William Shakespeare. Taurus the bull. The bull sees red, as you just did, Archie. This is Mrs. Stimpson, Archie. Fulvia, this is the gentleman I was speaking about earlier. The writer."

Archie said, "How do you do."

"Better, I dare say than you do," Mrs. Muckermann continued. "Mrs. Stimpson is a Virgo-Libra, born on the cusp, a minute after midnight on the twenty-third of September, combining Virgo's sharp analytical powers with Libra's idealism. A fascinating combination."

Mrs. Stimpson flashed a gratified smile and held up the wiggling dog. "And don't forget Thumper," she said. "Thumper's Aries, like Joan Crawford, Claire Boothe Luce and Harry Houdini. That's why he's so frisky."

Archie could think of nothing he wanted to say, and started to proceed to the dining room, when Mrs. Muckermann clamped her skinny fingers around his wrist. She said, "Even the weather seems to be conspiring against you tonight, poor boy. What seems like happenstance is all predestined . . . planned, a part of fate . . . But take precautions anyway: you know Gemini's alignment to the lungs. Don't catch cold tonight; it could easily develop into bronchitis."

"Thanks for caring," Archie said snidely.

"Oh, even though I do, I wonder if it matters," said Mrs. Muckermann. "I wonder if you haven't already turned down that road. I see you, symbolically, on a road in a storm such as the one outside, and then—" She shivered as the Yorkie did, removed her hand from his wrist and said, "Remember, Fulvia, what I told you about his configurations?"

And Fulvia nodded sadly.

"It was a pleasure meeting you like this," Archie told her, and left the pair looking after him as he journeyed to the double Dewar's and "Daddy" Gamble with his bride.


"Eleven o'clock," Archie said. "No answer out there."

Frank Gamble was staring out the window of the apartment on 18th Street, smoking a Dutch Masters and complaining, "We're never going to get off the ground in this soup!"

The eleven-thirty flight to San Juan had been canceled; they were standing by for a one-thirty possibility.

"Sometimes she doesn't answer the phone when she's this mad," said Archie, still standing under the Constitution mirror by the telephone stand. "I guess she's pulling that tonight."

"What's she so mad about?" said Liddy. She had kicked off her Guccis and she was rocking in the Boston Rocker, cradling a snifter filled with Remy Martin.

"She'd probably bought stuff for dinner . . . How the hell do I know what she's so mad about!" said Archie.

"Some women don't need a reason," Frank Gamble told him. "Your mother never did."

Archie laughed and picked up his beer. "If she didn't need them, it wasn't because they weren't in plentiful supply."

"Oh, dear God," Liddy groaned. "Are we going to start raking over your childhood again? I had fifteen years of that!"

"I didn't bring up the subject."

Frank Gamble said, "Well, it's time bygones were bygones."

"Then keep them bygone," Liddy said to him.

"I know I did things wrong," he said. "Hell, I hadn't had any practice being a father."

"Forget it," Archie said. "Drop it!"

"Son, I really appreciate the way you're taking this. Liddy and me. I really appreciate it."

"How'd you think I was going to take it?" said Archie, angry at himself for asking them back to the apartment.

"Frank thought you'd be after him with a gun," Liddy said. "He was even afraid to marry me in New York. He wanted me to get the damn Mexican divorce straightened out and then hop a plane to the Coast to get married. We were going to send you a postcard."

"I just wanted to be sure I wouldn't lose you, my darling," said Archie's father.

God, it was all so absurd and unbelievable. Archie was champing at the bit to tell Dru about it, when he wasn't champing at the bit to tell her off . . . Maybe they ought to have a baby if this behavior was any portent of the future; maybe they ought to have a chicken farm or a kennel or beehive or some damn thing that would keep her from concentrating all of her energies on him.

Could she have gone to a movie?

It was "Gala *Gone With The Wind* Week" at the local theater in Nyack, and they had seen it Tuesday night; that meant she would have had to drive to Spring Valley or New City . . . in this weather.

Liddy said, "Frank thought you'd hold up our divorce, Archie, that you wouldn't sign any of the papers. Honestly!"

"What would I have done with Dru?"

Frank Gamble said, "She doesn't think much of me, does she, son?"

"You can't win 'em all, Dad."

"Do I offend her? How do I offend her?"

"Naw—forget it."

"No, I want to know. I want us all to be friends."

Liddy kicked her leg up in the air and said, "Let's all live together, sleep in the same bed."

Archie laughed, but Frank Gamble was halfway into the bottle, fast approaching the middle ground between Maudlin and Inarticulate. His eyelids were starting to droop, and there was cigar ash on his vest. He said, "Does she hold it against me the way I treated your mother?"

"Why should she care?"

"Oh, you learn to care," Liddy said in a tone laced with irony, "if you prefer peace to war."

Archie said, "Come off it, Liddy. I never asked you to take sides."

"No, but what about that altar to Mother Gamble we had constructed in the living room?"

"Bullshit," Archie said.

"And all the votive candles with her initials on them?"

Archie's father lumbered across and poured himself another brandy. "Well," he said, "Archie's mother was a fine woman. A very decent woman. She really was."

"She really was," said Liddy. "I'm always hearing good things about her."

"Oh, can it, you two. The poor woman's dead; may she rest in peace." Archie looked at his watch. Eleven-ten.

Frank Gamble said, "Stop pot-watching. Watched pots never boil."

"If she knew I had to go to Bay Shore tomorrow, I wouldn't mind," Archie said.

Liddy lit a Gauloise. "She probably thinks you're tooting around with me."

"Oh, bank on that."

"You know what we ought to do," said Frank Gamble. "We ought to surprise Dru when we get back. Don't tell her anything about it, Archie. Just tell her Liddy's coming out with her new husband, and watch her face fall when she sees it's me."

Archie smiled weakly; he could see the possibilities in the idea as well as he could perceive anything that night. Clouding his perception right at that moment was his memory of Mrs. Muckermann's warning about his health and a vague sense of congestion in his chest. Was he imagining it? They had walked from the hotel in the pouring rain.

He said, "I'm going to try Dru again."

"Then I'll call the airlines," Frank Gamble said, "but we're not going to get anywhere in that soup out there. That's Campbell's soup and a half!"

Archie said, "What are you going to do if you have to stay over?"

"Find a hotel room," his father answered. "Liddy doesn't have a place any more, and my secretary's at my place with her boyfriend, baby-sitting for Woof-Woof."

"Woof-Woof," Liddy said affectionately. "My new step-poodle."

Archie said, "You can stay here. I'll sleep on the couch."

"There's something about that idea," said Liddy, "that's positively primal scene obscene."

"What's primal scene?" said Frank Gamble.

"Never mind," Liddy said, "or *you'll* start going to a shrink and then I'll lose all faith in human nature."

He didn't get Dru, and he didn't try after midnight. About that time Frank Gamble came wandering out of the bedroom, wearing one of Archie's old terrycloth robes, with his socks still strapped to his garters, and another Dutch Masters stuck into his jaw. Archie had fixed a bed on the couch. He was finishing a can of beer and a paperback reprint of a Patricia Highsmith suspense novel when Frank Gamble sat down heavily beside him.

"I really want to thank you, son, for making it so easy for Liddy and me. It means a lot."

"Don't mention it. You'd better get some sleep."

"You seem depressed, son. Did that astrologer back at the hotel depress you by telling you those things?"

"I was laughing when I told you about it. Didn't you see me laughing when I told you about it?"

"I know, son. Sometimes we laugh on the outside and cry on the inside."

Archie winced. "Dad, get some sleep."

"I will. But I want to tell you something."

"What's that?"

"Whatever your mother told you about me, son, I wish you'd stop and think about what I said earlier. I hadn't had any practice being a father."

"Let's just forget it, Dad. It doesn't matter."

"I'm a happy man now, son."

"I'm glad you are."

"And a happy man makes his peace with the world."

"I know."

"Gets things off his chest."

"Right."

"Airs things."

"Yeah. Right."

"A happy man wants everybody to be as happy a man as he is."

"Okay, Dad."

"I respected your mother, but I didn't really love her, son."

"Okay."

"She was a woman who commanded a man's respect."

"Fine."

"Now, I know she told you things about me. I never planned on having children. Whatever she told you, remember, son, I wasn't prepared for a child. One day your mother simply told me you were on the way."

"Sorry about that."

"I was flabbergasted, son. I was twenty years old, son. Just a boy myself. Just getting a start in life."

"Dad, you don't have to go into all of this. I don't care."

"The thing is: what'd your mother tell you?"

"About what?"

Liddy's voice then. "The thing is," said she, wearing Dru's yellow seersucker bathrobe, walking up to Frank Gamble, "you can't even sit up with the boys all night any more, Daddy Gamble, not even with your own boy. C'mon, Mommy wants you in with her."

She jerked him to his feet. Docilely, being led by the hand, Archie's father followed her into the bedroom.

Daddy Gamble and Mommy.

Jesus!

Eagerly, Archie returned to the utterly logical and predictable world of Miss Highsmith where: *Greg's hand was still free and plunging with the knife.*

C H A P T E R  23

"Hello, darling," she said.

"Hi there. No, wait—don't get in yet. I'm getting out."

"In the rain?"

"In the rain."

"And this fog—it's—"

"Coming in on little cat's feet," he said.

"Huh?"

"Once I drowned a cat. The runt of the litter."

"They're not like dogs. They're independent."

"Too independent."

"I guess so. This is a bad rain. Can't we get in the car?"

"Far too independent," he said.

"What have you got there? What are you carrying?"

"Forrest's gun."

"He doesn't own a gun . . . A *gun?*"

"This is his gun. I killed him with it."

"Hey, don't horse around. I don't like it."

"I put him in the *blue* Slumber Bag. Pink for girls; blue for boys."

"That *is* a gun!"

193

"That little cat was afraid, like your eyes are now. But she fought hard."

"Don't, Neal. I *am* afraid."

"You pushed Margaret, didn't you?"

"No! *No!*"

"You might as well admit it."

"I didn't push her!"

"Because it won't matter either way."

"Don't hurt my baby, Neal."

"It would only be another bad apple, Pen."

He fired the gun twice.

She fell to the ground near the right front wheel of the Falcon.

Her body was illuminated by the headlights from his Consul.

He tossed the revolver into the bushes, got back inside the Consul, removed his gloves and drove down the mountain. He listened to the radio announcer forecast clearing weather tomorrow and remembered all the times Penny and he had come up here this way in separate cars and felt this same fog come in the window of the Falcon, its cold dampness refreshing their warm bare flesh while they clung together in the back seat.

C H A P T E R  24

> And I thought of the albatross,
> And I wished he would come back, my snake.

While Neal Dana listened to Officer Baird on the phone, he smiled at the poem above his desk and at the naïveté which had prompted him to frame it and hang it there.

He had so many doubts about himself, hadn't he, before all of this had happened? He had been so self-chastising, so uncertain of his own mettle. Was it any wonder Margaret had ultimately cracked, and with the peculiar sense of the absurd characteristic of the mentally ill, chosen to look for support from someone altogether lacking in mettle?

"Clarence Bissel's coming by in an hour," said Baird. "He refuses to believe she was pregnant. He wants to see the autopsy report with his own eyes."

"Yes, he'd have that reaction," Neal said. "Penny was as afraid of having the baby because of him as she was afraid of not having it because of Forrest."

"She definitely said Forrest knew about it?"

"Yes."

"Then Forrest couldn't have been very far from here."

"Unless he called her long distance. Penny claimed she had no idea where he was."

"She wouldn't have admitted it if she did know."

"I suppose not."

"And she gave no indication who fathered the child?"

"She said he was a stranger. She hadn't seen him before or after she met him that night at the drive-in."

"Had she actually approached anyone about performing an abortion, Dr. Dana?"

Neal said, "I don't think so. What she really wanted from me yesterday was a confirmation that abortion wasn't a sin. I said it wasn't a matter of it being a sin, it was a matter of risking her health, if not her life."

"What was her reaction?"

"She seemed to want to take the risk. She didn't know how to go about it, though—who to ask."

"So I suppose she asked Forrest; who else could she turn to for help with something like that?"

"I don't know."

"She asked Forrest, and Forrest argued with her."

"Yes, according to her he would have tried to talk her out of it."

"And kill her when he wasn't able to."

"That's hard to believe."

"Is it, Dr. Dana? I think Forrest was somewhere in the vicinity. He met her up on the mountain to talk with her about this. There was an argument. He shot her . . . Incidentally, we're combing the mountains for any trace of him . . . and Mrs. Dana."

"Yes . . . I don't think of Forrest as a killer."

"A killer isn't thought of as a killer, until he kills."

"Still . . ."

"We traced the gun, Dr. Dana. It belongs to a fellow named Fitzhugh. He worked with Forrest; they were buddies. Fitzhugh's in the hospital with hernia trouble, been there two weeks."

"Then that pretty much says it," said Neal.

The policeman said, "Yes, that says it."

Neal returned to examining the folder of a patient suffering from alcoholic psychosis. He studied his Wechsler-Bellevue, Wells Memory Test, and Stanford-Binet Vocabulary findings.

He had never worked with more assiduity; he had never realized such interior calm.

Last night he had slept more soundly than he had since he was a very young man. He had awakened remembering a dream which truly spelled out his metamorphosis. In it, Rachmaninoff's *Rhapsody on a Theme of Paganini* was playing, and his father was dancing with a golden statue who was carrying an ear of corn. When Neal went to cut in, Margaret said: "How's that little girl whose brother you helped?" Norman Dana laughed. "Neal's the little girl, aren't you, Cornelia?", and Neal pumped three bullets into his heart. Then he buried him.

"May I ask you something?" Margaret said. "Do you want plain squash or squash with onions and tomatoes?"

And then he ran toward Margaret through the tall elephant grass, smelled the scent of the sun in her hair when he caught her to him; her fingers held on to his shirt, both of them laughing so hard.

Neal's father had been dead since Neal was a freshman in college, but Neal could remember when he was a student coming across a sentence of Desnoyers: *"Ce sont les morts qu'il faut qu'on tue."* One must kill the dead. Neal had underlined it, memorized it, but never learned to do it. Look there for the reason he found it necessary to frame such poems as the one hanging above his desk.

Until Neal had buried him, finally, last night, Norman Dana had survived the grave, was the reason Neal had never found the confidence to study medicine, and the reason, too, these past few days, for the paranoia which had compelled Neal to imagine Margaret had been with many men besides Forrest Bissel.

One must kill the dead.

And now Margaret ran toward him in dreams, younger and laughing, with her hair spilling to her shoulders, and lived in fantasies while Neal listened to music or drove to work or sat on the upper porch under the stars watching the lights of the Tappan Zee.

Margaret lived, and so she should, for she had never wanted anything for Neal but what was best, and she had given him her best until the very end, when his inadequacies finally took their toll from her.

Neal flipped through the pages in the file until he found the patient's Rorschach. He studied it, noted the impairment of the visual-motor functioning and the absence of response to the bright color area, and then he glanced at his watch.

It was four-thirty.

He slipped the file into his briefcase (Margaret, with her unfailing good taste, had found it for him at Mark Cross) and buzzed his secretary to announce that he was leaving for the day.

On his way home he stopped to buy a newspaper. The headline was devoted to the President's speech, but at the bottom of the front page Neal saw: LOCAL GIRL KILLED IN MOUNTAINS.

Dru Gamble was sitting in the Cages' Buick waiting for Neal when his car came up the hill. In the back seat she had two suitcases which she had spent the afternoon packing; in the pocket of her rust-colored linen suit, the train schedule from Tarrytown with the departure time circled and the time of arrival in Syracuse checked.

She was carrying the letters and the diary, and her own letter to Neal, as she got out of the Buick and greeted him.

"Hi! How about a swim? I think it's warm enough," he said.

"Only if you'll promise to drown me."

"Hey, Dru, what's the matter?"

"Name it."

"Oh, nothing's that bad. Let me fix you a drink."

She tried to think of things that would keep the tears behind the floodgates as she followed him into the house. She had made up her mind not to discuss her problems with Neal; that would be colossal nerve considering her reason for being there, but three sips through her martini it all came out. She told him how the answering service had called to advise her that Archie had to leave for Long Island early that morning on business, and how she had decided to go to New York for the weekend—let Archie fend for himself out here. She told him of her arrival at the apartment. She described the bed made up on the living-room couch, the dents in both pillows of the double bed in the bedroom, and the Gauloises in the ashtray on the bed table.

"It sounds like he slept on the couch," Neal said.

"He probably started out on the couch. That would be Archie's way. Stay over, he'd say, I'll sleep on the couch."

"Look, Dru, if Archie had gone in to see her yesterday, and for the reason you say, and if she's the sort you describe, why would there have been any reason for him to make up the couch? They would have just gone to bed in the first place, wouldn't they?"

"Archie didn't know *why* he was going into New York yesterday. I'm sure he thought it was business. Then a sudden impulse overtook him, right? To call Liddy. Oh, I know him. If he'd planned it, he would have stayed at Liddy's."

"That was a bad storm last night. Remember that."

"I know. That was probably the excuse. He probably invited her to our place, and then persuaded her not to go home because of the storm. Then another sudden impulse overtook him, right? He got up from the couch and moved stealthily toward the bedroom. Lurching, no doubt, from wall to wall.

I know he was loaded."

"How do you know that?"

"He was smoking cigars. He has to be loaded to the gills for that."

She told him she was going to her sister's in Syracuse, and Neal said he'd drive her to Tarrytown to the train.

"*Maybe* you will," said Dru.

"No. I will. I don't think you should go without hearing Archie's side, but if you're determined, I'll drive you there."

"See how you feel when you look this over," said Dru.

She stood up and walked across to the coffee table in front of the couch. She put the letters and the diary on it, and her letter to Neal. Neal picked up the pack of letters from Tuto first.

"Letters of Margaret's?"

"Letters of Margaret's," said Dru. "You might as well take a look, Neal. And there's a letter there from me."

She left him puzzling over it all, took the newspaper from atop his briefcase, and went back to the wing chair by the window. A warm breeze blew the curtains; yes, it was warm enough today to swim, and she imagined Archie and Liddy boarding the ferry in Bay Shore early that morning for the ride across to Ocean Beach.

Business in Bay Shore.

Archie ought to have been able to come up with something better than that.

Bay Shore was Fire Island. Period. It was Ocean Beach, or Point O' Woods, or Fair Harbor, or Saltaire, or Kismet, but it was Fire Island.

What other reason was there for anyone to go to Bay Shore?

Dru heard Neal mutter "Diable," under his breath.

She fortified herself with a large swallow of martini, and shook the fold from the Rockland-Orange *Gazette*.

She said, "Neal? Before you read any more, would you read my letter to you first?"

Then Dru turned her attention to the newspaper.

### LOCAL GIRL KILLED
### IN MOUNTAINS

Penny Bissel, 22, of 2102 Main Street, Nyack, New York was found dead late last night beside a Ford Falcon registered in the name of Clarence Bissell, her father.

Miss Bissell had been shot twice, through the heart, with a small Browning automatic pistol.

Autopsy was performed revealing the victim was pregnant.

The lonely road on Bear Mountain where the body was discovered by state troopers is a popular lovers' . . .

Three words ripped across her mind like whiplashes.

*Penny!*

*Falcon!*

*Pregnant!*


Dru Gamble looked up from the newspaper at the same time Neal Dana put her letter down on the coffee table.

Their eyes met.

He was the first to move. He stood.

And to speak. "I'm sorry, Dru."

Then he came slowly toward her.

CHAPTER 25

A yellow bee flew into the back seat of the Buick.

Tiffany Cage, a curled beige ball on the floor, lazily removed a dark brown paw from one crossed blue eye, and peered up in the direction of the buzzing.

The bee swooped down and made a pass at her nose, desperately trying to find a way out of the Buick.

Tiffany Cage sniffed with irritation, opened the other crossed eye, and snapped the air angrily with her crooked dark brown tail.

The bee circled overhead and made another pass, tickling the cat's ear with its wings.

Tiffany Cage hissed and rose on her haunches.

The bee brushed by her whiskers.

Tiffany Cage made an outraged swipe at the air.

The bee persisted, circling, swooping down, buzzing, touching the cat's fur.

Tiffany Cage leaped out the car window in a fury.

For a moment she sat licking her paw comfortingly while her tail flagged behind her; then she gave a surly look around her, and surefootedly stalked slowly toward the woods in a terrible feline rage.

Asleep on the rock near the woodshed, the rock still warm from the afternoon sun, the blacksnake stirred suddenly. His forked tongue darted rapidly as he raised his head and held it still as a tree twig on a breezeless day. He waited. Warned and sensing something from some movement unnatural to the wind, he dropped with a soft hissing-scrape into the dry leaves beneath the rock.

His long body rowed the earth, every scale an oar, biting the dirt with the ridges of his body as he sought the deep fissure among the rocks out of which he had wandered.

The leaves behind him rustled.

The winding stream of his length contorted to a twisted arrow as he lashed through the grass like a cast lance.

The cat's paw pressed him captive to the dust; her fangs found his wiggling neck and lifted him deftly, running with him from the woods, mercilessly refusing to murder him.

She skirted the swimming pool, dancing excitedly through the grass and across the gravel, watching the house for a way to enter.

She saw the open window and galloped smartly with the blacksnake hanging from her mouth, dragging along the path by the side of the house.

Tiffany Cage crouched, measured the distance from the ground to the windowsill, then jumped it expertly.

She paused, and saw a shoulder, leaped and perched atop the shoulder as it was bent over a chair, and deposited her gift across the flesh of a neck.

A piercing scream frightened the cat, who had never heard that sound from a man.

Tiffany Cage beat it back to the Buick, leaving the blacksnake behind her.

Footsteps then, running. The car door opened, closed.

The woman made the car go.

CHAPTER 26

On the Fourth of July, Archie and Dru Gamble made Rum Runners and a barbecue in the Cages' backyard for Frank and Liddy Gamble.

Tiffany was there, too, fatter than she'd ever been before as a consequence of Dru Gamble's obsessive indulgence. She occupied a zebra-striped director's chair close to the barbecue pit, patiently tolerating the noise around her as she napped between juicy snacks of charcoaled sirloin.

Night fell and the fireflies flew around twinkling brightly like the blanket of stars overhead, and Liddy got too high to find her Guccis in the grass beneath the hammock, so Dru searched for them while Frank Gamble drew his son aside and once again began, "I hope we're friends, good friends."

"With an astro-twin like I have, I need all the friends I can get," Archie replied.

Liddy was lounging in the hammock, waving a Gauloise at the mosquitoes. "Astro-twin, smashtro-twin, so long as you love your mother . . . and your daddy. Right, Frank?"

"I'm trying to be serious with my son," said Frank Gamble. "A man ought to be able to have a heart-to-heart talk with his own son in private."

"You said it, Judge Hardy," said Liddy.

Dru asked, "Who's Judge Hardy?"

Archie groaned. "My child bride."

"Oh, shut up," said Dru. "I'm not your bride any more, I'm your wife. I hate all these annoying little funnies about our marriage, and I hate the word 'judge,' and I also hate the word 'lawyer,' and 'policeman'—"

"And wanna bet you don't miss a day in court when they try Neal?"

"If I'm *alive*," said Dru.

"That's right," Archie said. "Remember what Mrs. Muckermann said."

"What'd she say?" Liddy said.

"She thinks Dru's doomed," said Archie.

"Well," Frank Gamble said, "the lesson in this whole thing is that astrology's a lot of bunk. I never doubted it, and I'd be the first to accept it, if it made any sense at all. I'm an Aquarian, after all, and this is supposed to be the great Aquarian age. A lot of very impressive people were Aquarians, I'm told. Franklin Roosevelt and Abraham Lincoln, Douglas MacArthur, and Galileo."

Liddy said, "I think you're a lot like Galileo, Frank."

"It's a lot of bunk and I never doubted it," he said, "but when I heard Archie was getting involved in that special, I told myself oh oh."

"Oh oh?" said Liddy. "Oh oh good or oh oh bad?"

"Oh oh watch out, is what I told myself, because Archie here is inclined to go overboard, get too intense about things. Get an idea in his head and never get it out of his head."

"Like the idea he doesn't love his daddy," said Liddy. "Here we go again."

Frank Gamble said, "No, I've said my last word on that subject. We're good friends now, aren't we, Archie?"

"The best. Will you loan me a few thousand, pal?"

"You're making more than I make. How much are they paying you for that special?"

"Ten thow."

"Ten thousand dollars for a few months' work! All that money for a show about a lot of bunk."

"It might surprise you, Dad."

"It won't surprise me, because I won't watch bunk. Sports is the only thing I watch on the TV. Sports and Huntley and Brinkley."

Dru said, "It is going to be fascinating, Father Gamble. The dear Lord knows I'd be the last person to give any support to astrology, but CBS did find these astro-twins who are so much alike it's as though Mrs. Muckermann invented them."

"They're Aquarians, too," said Archie. "They can practically finish each other's sentences they're so much alike."

"You stand there and say that, when the man who's your astro-twin is an admitted murderer?"

Dru said, "Please let's not talk about Neal. I don't want to talk about Neal."

"Then you do think there's something in all this, ah?" Frank Gamble said.

"No," Dru said, "I don't. That isn't why I don't want to talk about him. I was fond of him, that's why. I still am."

"Anyway," said Archie, "there's a little something in everything, Dad. There's something in numerology, phrenology, ESP. It doesn't work for most people, but for some by God it does. You don't buy it all, but you don't turn your back on all of it either."

"I do, son. God's good enough for me."

"Are you good enough for Him, though, Frank?" Liddy said.

"I've made my peace."

"And you're ready to die now? Are you trying to tell me something, old daddy?"

Dru said, "Here's your other shoe. Let's stop talking about death. Please."

"Here's your hat," said Liddy. "What's your hurry?"

"I didn't mean it that way, Liddy. I don't want you to go. I hate it when people leave before midnight. What'd we get drunk for, to go to bed?"

"It helps," Liddy said.

Frank Gamble said, "No, we can't stay. We've got to get back while I can still drive."

Liddy sat up and put on her shoes. "Scorpio's rising," she said.

Frank Gamble tried to draw Archie aside. He said, "Son, whatever your mother—"

"*I'm* Archie's mother now," Liddy said, "and I want to go home, Daddy-O."

Firecrackers exploded over the New York skyline as they approached the George Washington Bridge.

Liddy handed Frank Gamble two quarters for the toll.

"Stop trying to tell Archie about it, Frank," she said. "He doesn't know about it. Leave it that way."

"He might know about it. His mother was always crying on his shoulder."

"Wouldn't I know if he knew? *He* was always crying on my shoulder."

"I want him to like me."

"He's not going to like you if you tell him that he was born in the back of a taxi on the way to the hospital."

"I keep thinking his mother told him. If she did, I'd like to say something about it. Not just leave it go . . . His mother never forgave me that, you know. She was humiliated having to go to the hospital by herself that way."

"Water over the dam, Frank."

"When you get on in years, my darling, you look back at

yourself, and some things you did you never forgive yourself for."

"I gather."

"I don't even remember, any more, the name of the lady I was with."

"Polly Adler maybe?"

"But I had a feeling all the while I was with her that something was wrong at home. I finally called. When there was no answer, I telephoned Dr. MacNeice."

"Well, you got there, Frank. Don't be so hard on yourself."

"I got there at three-thirty. My son was already crying. I could hear him crying all the way down the hall. It scared the hell out of me, Liddy. I was twenty years old, and I was a father." He turned onto the bridge. "The nurse went inside and held my son up to the window so I could see him. He was just two hours old. Did you ever see a two-hour-old baby?" He laughed. "He looked like a little—*I* don't know."

"Gemini?" Liddy said.

CHAPTER 27

On May 27, 1927, at one-thirty A.M., the sun was in Gemini. The rising sign was Pisces.